ANXIETY IN A STARBUCKS CUP

ALYSHA JUGUAN

Contents

"Come on!" Leanne yells in frustration. She has been trying to refresh the page of her social media accounts for the past thirty minutes, but nothing came out, only a blank screen. Frustrated, she throws her phone beside her. Screw this internet data. No matter how expensive the data is, if the network sucks, it sucks.

She was in the middle of stalking her long-time crush, Ethan De Ruine when her screen froze. Her hot sexy Hispanic man, he's not hers, but she is claiming him as hers in her dreams (a girl can dream, can't she?), whom she's been stalking since her freshman year in college.

Leanne can remember all too well how she met Ethan. It was the first day of class, an orientation day, as they all call it, and there he was with the other higher years. He was one of the speakers, encouraging the freshmen into Mechanical Engineering because it was supposed to be *fun*, but we all know Engineering is far from fun.

The way he talks captured Leanne's attention. He talks smart, and his voice demands attention. If he was a sales representative, Leanne would have bought everything he was selling. Since then, she was stalking him, silently.

Leanne frowned when the page finally refreshed, and the photo of Ethan and his girlfriend of six months popped up. They were smiling at the camera that the girl was holding, with the beach as their backdrop. Does she feel jealous? Hell, yes. These girls have been so lucky to be his girlfriends. The woman in the photo has been his fifth girlfriend since he graduated.

Leanne sigh when the page freezes again. "Stupid, piece of shit," she cursed at her phone.

She glances at the time on her watch to see that it's two in the afternoon, still enough time before her shift. With the way, the internet is acting might as well use Wi-Fi.

"I need coffee," she murmurs while she gets dressed. But she already had one for breakfast. The doctor limited her to one cup per day. Who drinks one cup of coffee a day? She has no qualms with tea, it's just that tea tastes different than the black coffee that she is accustomed to.

The nearest Starbucks is ten minutes away by car, considering she doesn't have one, walking was not an option. She booked her Uber while she was fixing all the stuff that she must bring. She double-checks her bag just to make sure that her notebook is inside.

That notebook is her lifeline. It's where her skeletons are hidden. If others hide them in their closet, she hides them in her notebook. That is why she never left her notebook. If her friends find the notebook, then all her skeletons are out.

"Good afternoon, Ma'am!" one of the Starbucks' baristas, who is mopping the floor greets her.

She nods her head in acknowledgment before inhaling the scent of the coffee that lingers around the café. This is the closest she can get to her cup of coffee. If only she knew that she'll be in Starbucks, she wouldn't have that coffee during breakfast. Why must the good things be prohibited to her? Like, seriously?

"Hello, ma'am!" the barista greets her with a smile. "May I take your order?"

"Umm … one hibiscus tea with pomegranate pearls," she says while grabbing her wallet from her bag. "Venti."

The barista punches in her order while she hands her the money. "Is that all, ma'am?"

She nods and waits for her change. "What would be the name for the cup?" the barista asks her with her sharpie in one hand while holding a clear Venti cup on the other.

"Leanne," she says, knowing that the barista would mess up her name one way or the other. She's used to it anyway.

"We'll call out your order, ma'am," the barista smiles while handling her receipt. "Have a nice day!"

She nods in answer and heads to the station where she would grab her drink. She scans the crowd hoping to find a vacant table. To her disappointment, there is none. She glances at the second floor hoping that there is at least a chair available.

Leanne fishes out her phone when she heard a chime. It was just a message from their group chat, saying that their lead tech would be absent due to personal reasons. She sighs and ignores the message even though her fingers itch to reply to a smartass comeback.

It's her last day at work, and she just wants to relax, but all of a sudden, her lead tech decided that it's a good time to go YOLO. She hates being the acting lead tech. Too much stress. Damn, she needs that coffee ASAP.

"Order for Ma'am Li-anne!"

She glances up when she heard her name being called out, but she didn't move to grab her drink, instead, she waited for the barista to call out her name again. Hoping that they might pronounce it right.

"Order for Ma'am Li-anne!"

Nope. She shouldn't have hoped. They always pronounce her name wrong. It's Lee-yan. A softer version of Li-anne. She sighs and goes ahead to grab her drink. People always pronounce her name wrong. She's used to it anyway. At first, it would irritate her, and she would correct them. But as years goes by, she decided to screw it. Pronounce it however you want, she doesn't care anymore.

She heads up to the second floor of the café, and thank the gods there is a vacant chair at the farthest corner of the room, far away from the crowd. Just how she likes it. She drops her bag on the seat beside her and gets herself comfortable. She knows that she's going to be here for quite some time.

"Dude," Vince says to his friend on the phone. "Just order me a coffee without any whipped cream."

"They all have whipped cream!" his friend says on the other line.

Vince rolls his eyes while looking for a spot to park his car. He should have had an order for them both and saved them all the hassle in ordering a freaking coffee. "A café latte, you piece of shit. You act like you haven't even tried to order in Starbucks."

"Shut up," his friend grumble and repeat his order to the barista. "Have you parked already?"

"I'm going to go around again," he says, driving the car around. "I'll see if there is an empty parking lot near the entrance."

"' mkay."

Vince ends the call and quickly parks the car in the available space just in front of the door. Just his luck. He locks the car and heads inside the café. He opens the door and steps aside when a person suddenly dashes, almost knocking him out.

"Sorry," he hears her murmur. Yes, it's she.

He looked back and saw her red hair tips flipping and waving as she speed-walks towards the other side of the road, towards a waiting car. He shrugs it off. Maybe she's running late? He sees Deo waiting for their drinks, and he gestures that he's going to find them a seat.

He heads to the upper floor since all the seats on the ground floor are taken. He just found the table that he wants, at the farthest corner of the café. Knowing his friend, he will not drag him to have coffee just because he feels like it. Something is bothering Deo. He had an idea about what is it all about, but he wants to hear it from his friend.

He's about to sit down when he sees a pastel green notebook on the floor. Reluctantly, he grabs it and sees that it was the 2019 Starbucks planner. He turns the planner around to see if there is a name written by the cover. But there is none. He sits down and removes the strap that seals the planner shut, he was hoping for a name, contact info, or anything that could lead him to the owner of the planner, but the first page is blank. He flips through the pages of the planner and sees that it is filled with writing, poem, stories, and random scribbles. Is this a diary?

He doesn't want to impose on the privacy of the owner, but he must find out who owns this planner so that he can return it. He's sure that the owner must be already in a panic since he/she couldn't find their planner. He flips the pages until he reaches the last entry.

Like a fool, I've watched you,

Silently hoping that you'll look at me too.

How naïve. How stupid I've been,

> ***For wishing something far from***

reach.

Vince feels like he was violating the person's privacy by reading the first four lines of the poem, but he now knows that the owner of the planner is a girl. Based on the handwriting, of course. The handwriting is too feminine for it to belong to a guy.

"What are you reading?"

Vince snaps the planner shut. He's already snooping on the privacy of the owner, and it's not nice to show something that doesn't belong to you. He strapped the planner shut and place it on the table in front of him.

"That is none of your business now, Deo," he says as he grabs his drink from his friend.

"Really? Come on, man. Share something."

Deo sits in front of him and tries to grab the planner, but he's fast enough to move it away from his friend's reach. "This isn't yours to read."

"But yours to read?" Deo sends him a smirk and slurps on his drink loudly, enough to make the other tables look at him in disgust.

Vince rolls his eyes and sips on his drink, quietly. "I'm just figuring out who the owner is."

"Oh, really?" his friend taunts him. "You aren't a bit curious on what is in that notebook—"

"Planner."

"What?" Deo pauses confused but soon realized that he was being corrected. "Planner, notebook, whatever. Aren't you a little bit curious? The owner wouldn't know if you get to read a snippet of what's on that planner."

He doesn't want to give Deo satisfaction by saying yes. He is tempted. He only read just a few sentences, and it made him want to flip the notebook and read it from the beginning. Not because he wants to find out who the owner is but because he's curious. This is the part where he's going to be killed because of the saying 'Curiosity kills the cat.' He's the cat, and the curiosity of what's inside the planner is killing him.

But a part of him is saying that whatever is in that notebook wasn't meant to be ready with anybody.

"I'm not curious at all." He maintained a straight face because one crack on his expression and his friend will find out that he is lying. "I'm simply skimming to see if there is any contact information of the owner."

"Uh-huh," his friend sends him a knowing look. Not buying his lie. "Whatever floats your boat?"

Vince glares at him and changes the subject. "You didn't drag me here just to talk about the planner, isn't it?"

Deo coughs when the coffee goes down the wrong pipe. "What made you think that there is a reason why I asked you to coffee? I just want to meet my friend. We haven't been hanging out lately."

He frowns. It's been two years since they last hangout as a group. If he remembers it correctly, it was during Taylor's bachelor party. After that wild night and the wedding, they went on their separate ways. Now that Deo mentioned it, he kind of misses hanging out with the guys.

"Is that really the reason?" He pushes. "I'm sure we can call them right now for a coffee, but you only called me. Now, Deo, spill it. What do you need?"

"What made you think that?"

"Your tone." He waves a hand in the air. "The way you are stalling the conversation."

Deo chuckles. "You got me. Well…"

He raises an eyebrow in his direction when he trails off. "Spill it, or I will call Dianne."

"Fuck off," Deo scowls when he mentioned Deo's sister's name. "My parents are making me meet a 'potential bride' again."

"That's like the second this month." He sips the last remaining coffee. "Don't your parents get tired?"

Deo looks at him like he grew a second head out of nowhere. "Dude, my family's Chinese. Being arranged to be married is like the sole duty, and the reason why you were born."

Vince winced at the words Deo said. He pities his friend sometimes. Deo had been arranged to be married ever since he reached the age of twenty. However, his first arrangement got canceled because the girl was caught in a relationship with someone else. Deo was ecstatic, but that was cut short when his parents, after three months, found him another bride. He knows his friend. He can't defy his parents, it's like an Asian thing. That is rule number one or the golden rule in an Asian family; never defy or embarrass your parents.

He and Deo grew up together. He met Deo during their pre-school years. Deo was a chubby kid back then. Fat cheeks and chubby arms are often subject to bullies, and Deo was always the receiving end of those bullies. Vince grew up with two older siblings, and he knows what a bully is since his siblings love to bully him every chance they got.

Vince found Deo one time crying and eating alone in their classroom. His white uniform turned into a dirty kind of yellow and clings to his skin. His best guess was that one of the bullies poured or threw his juice pack on Deo, and that pissed Vince off. The following day, he caught them on the act, taking Deo's packed lunch and dumping it in the trashcan.

He didn't know where he got the strength or courage, but he threw a might punch on one of the bullies' faces and kicked the other on the shin. From then on, they were inseparable.

"I can't make up any other excuses anymore, Vince," Deo sigh and run his hand through his hair. "She just graduated last week, and now my parents and her parents want us to get married next month! I mean— I don't even know her!"

"That's because you would always ditch her when you have to meet her for dinner or lunch," he states as a matter of fact. "Why don't you give her a chance? She's actually not that bad."

"Then why don't you marry her instead?"

Vince chuckles stand up and pat Deo on the shoulders. "As far as I can remember. I'm not Deo Lim. Why should I marry her?"

He laughs when he hears his friend groan. He glances at the notebook sitting at the car seat beside him. He frowns. Time to search for the owner then.

Leanne lets out a loud groan when she feels her muscles and joints pop. Finally, after twelve hours of straight work, she can go home. Just imagining her bed made her hazy with sleep. She hates it the most when she's on night duty. Damn, she didn't even grab a douse of sleep.

"Hey, Leanne." She looks up from her computer to see her co-worker, May, standing in front of her. "We're going to grab a meal before heading home. Are you going to join us?"

She shakes her head no. "I'm so sleepy, May. Raincheck?"

"Come on!" Sally butts from her right. "It's your rest day already. Having a meal won't hurt."

If she isn't dead tired, she has had accepted the offer, but she's so exhausted that eating is the last thing on her mind. She can barely think properly. "I'll pass. I'm hammered."

They shrug and leave her alone, knowing that she won't change her mind. Leanne quickly sends the last mail that needs to be sent and clocks out of the company. She frowns when the sun suddenly blinds her. She forgets to bring her cap again.

The travel from the company to her apartment is only forty-five minutes. She doesn't even bother changing her clothes, she drops to her bed and closes her eyes. Some time, while she was dozing off, she suddenly remembered her notebook and panicked. Sleep suddenly isn't her priority as she grabs her bag from the floor and sees that her notebook isn't there.

Calm down, Leanne, she told herself. *Think. Where was the last time you left it?* The office? She grabs her phone and dials Anne, her roommate and co-worker in the company.

"Hello?" She answers on the third ring.

"Anne! Did I leave a green notebook in the office?" She tries to sound calm and collected, but the panic in her voice is evident.

"No, there is no notebook here."

Shit. "Thanks."

She drops the call and starts to pace back and forth. Right before she heads to the company, she stopped by Starbucks. She remembered placing the notebook in her bag before she left the café. Did she leave it there? Sweet mother of Zeus, how can she be so careless?

She quickly changes her clothes and head to Starbucks that she visited yesterday. She feels her panic rise to her throat when the thought of someone reading her notebook aside from her suddenly pops into her mind. Let's not go there. Let it be there, she prays repeatedly. She needed that notebook.

She says a quick greeting to the barista who opens the door for her and heads straight to the table where she sat yesterday. She felt her anxiety rise ten-fold when she doesn't see a notebook.

"Excuse me," she asks the group who are currently sitting at the table. "Do you happen to notice a notebook on this table?"

They all shake their head no. She feels like throwing up. *Calm down, Leanne.* She tells herself. Maybe someone left it on the counter in case she came back? She heads downstairs and ignores the glares of the people lining up when she moves her way to the front.

"Excuse me," she cut off the person who's about to order.

"Miss, there is a line," the lady snaps at her.

"Just a sec," she murmurs at the lady and turns to the frowning barista, who is displeased with her cutting the line. "Did someone leave or hide a notebook here? It is a green Starbucks planner. Did someone leave it here?"

"I'm sorry, miss," the barista says. "Nobody saw a notebook."

"But—"

"She said that there is no notebook!" The lady interrupts. She is so close to banging this lady onto the display counter. "Now, move along!"

The barista sighs and looks at her. "There is no notebook. I'm sorry, but you need to leave."

She doesn't have to be told twice. She runs her hands through her hair in frustration. How can she be so careless? She squats at an empty parking area and takes a deep breath to calm herself. Where could her notebook be?

She feels her throat clog up with unshed tears. She is so sure that she won't lose her notebook that she didn't bother writing any contact information in case she would lose it. Now, her worst fears came true. She lost her notebook.

Vince looks up from the line when he hears a commotion in front. From what he sees, a woman cut in front of the line and is currently having a conversation with the barista. He glances at his watch to see that he has only forty-five minutes before his class starts.

He sees a distraught woman pass by him. He saw the panic in her eyes despite the brave face that she put up, and the green Starbucks planner suddenly comes into his mind. Well, not everyone who came into the café is the owner of the planner, not all distraught panicking woman who owns a green planner who happens to lose it. Not everyone. But maybe…

He snaps his attention when he hears a cough. He looks up and sees that it was his turn to order. "Café Latte, please," He decides to ask the barista about the woman. "What was that commotion about earlier?"

"Oh," The barista looks up from the cashier. "She was asking if someone left a notebook here."

"What?" Vince said, shock. Who knew?

The barista shrugs, unaware of the shock that he's in. Of all the coincidences... "What would be the name, sir?"

"Cancel it," he says and quickly dashes outside, hoping that the woman still hasn't left the area.

He heads to his car to grab the notebook and search for her. He isn't sure if she was still around the vicinity since a few minutes has passed already when she left the café. He has no idea who he is looking for, all he knows is that he's searching for a woman. It can, again, be anyone. He is searching for almost five minutes, and still no sign of her anywhere.

Disappointed with the opportunity missed, he decides to head back to his car. He still has a class to teach anyway. He stops, a few meters away from him is a woman with red-hair tips, squatting and rocking back and forth. This was the woman yesterday, who almost bumped into him. He searched everywhere but not in the parking lot. It never crossed his mind to search for her there.

Clutching the planner, Vince walks slowly towards her, afraid that he might startle her or scare her away. He is about to tap her when he hears her murmuring and sniffing.

"It's okay," He hears her utter to herself while patting her shoulders. "You...you can buy another one. It's not lost. Y-you ju-just have to calm down, Leanne."

He knew that technique that she was doing. He often recommends to it his patients, the butterfly hugs. It's a technique used to calm or relax an anxious or panicked mind. It makes them think that someone is comforting them. He sighs and walks to stand in front of her. He tries to look at her face, but her hair covers her whole face, and she doesn't bother to move it.

"I can still find it." She nods to what she's saying. "I...I just have to calm down."

"Miss?" he whispers and holds the notebook in front of her. "I heard you were looking for this?"

She looks up, and he holds his breath when a pair of brown eyes meet his. They were the darkest color of brown that he has ever seen, and it fascinates him. He knows that they lighten up when she laughs or smiles, and he hasn't even seen her smile. He just knows.

But the eyes that are staring at him right now, aren't light and bright, they are dull and lifeless. Her eyes move from him to the planner that he is holding, in a snap, the dullness in her eyes fills with relief, but they aren't still as bright as he wanted them to be. What the fuck is going with him?

"Oh my gosh." She stands up so suddenly that she trips on her own feet. She would have hit the floor, but he managed to grab her.

Leanne stops as if time stopped as well. To say that he is handsome would be an understatement. She can feel her breath hitch when his eyes meet hers. They aren't dark, nor they are light. They just seem to be in the middle shade of brown. His eyes are so expressive that they made her want to cower away and hide, but at the same time, she wants to read and experience them all.

What amazes her the most is how calm she is right now. It is a sudden onslaught of calmness that caught her off guard and she want to cling to it a little longer.

As if he's aware that she was checking him out, he smirks at her. She pulls away from him and can stand properly on her own. Not that she is against being held by him but... The notebook!

She turns to him and grabs the notebook from his hands. She flips through the pages and lets out a sigh of relief when she sees that everything is still intact, no missing notebook pages and no unnecessary scribbles that doesn't belong to her.

"I know that notebook is important to you, that's why I didn't leave it at the café," he says.

She sends a forced smile at him. "Thank you, but next time if you found something that isn't yours, might as well leave it at the counter of the café."

He shrugs the sudden irritation at the way she smiled at him and smiles at her instead. "As curious as I am as to what is inside that notebook, I didn't read it."

She stares at him. Reading him. "You sure?"

He nods, places three fingers on his chest, and drags it downwards, starting below his collarbone and ending on his heart. At first, Leanne thought that he made an Ancient Greek gesture to ward off evil spirits and bad lucks, but then realizes that she had no idea why he did that gesture.

"What did you just do?" she asks him.

"Oh, that?" he repeats the gesture. "I do that when I make a promise."

"Oh..." She nods. "That's cute."

"Cute?" He looks at her like she grew another head. "It's far from cute."

He feels bad that he swore to her that he didn't read the notebook. He did read a part of it. He can't help it. He wants to know more about the person who wrote it but seeing her eyes light up when he said and swore that he didn't read it made him even guiltier of hiding it from her.

A breath of laugh escapes her, and Vince's breath just stops when he hears that sound. It was a split-second teasing scoff and it bring warm flutters into his guts. He wants to hear it again. He'll do anything to hear that sound again, but reality must remind him of his responsibility.

He glances at his watch and sees that he only has ten minutes if there is no traffic, and all the stoplights are green before class starts. "Hey, um … I have to get going. I still have a class to teach."

Oh? So, he's a teacher? Leanne nods at him and clutches the notebook closer to her chest. "Thank you for returning my notebook. It means so much to me."

He smiles. A genuine smile reaches his eyes, making the dimple on his checks show. "I know."

Leanne stares at him. Not wanting him to leave yet, she feels safe with him, and she doesn't hear any voices in her head even though they are two arms apart from one another. "See you around?"

He nods and turns away from her. *It's now or never, Leanne! Ask for his number!* One voice in her head says. *Are you insane?* The second one says. *He's a stranger!* A hot stranger. She had so many opportunities missed because of the what-ifs in her mind. Before her anxiety swallows her, she calls his attention.

"Hey!"

Vince looks back when he heard her call him. "Yeah?" He stops and places his hands on his pockets, watching her walk towards him.

"Um..." She tightens her hold on the notebook as if it offers her the strength that she needed. "If it's too much to ask..."

"Yes?" Vince shifts from one foot to the other, nervous about what she's going to say.

Leanne sigh and grab her phone from her bag. She holds her phone towards him. "Can I have your number?"

He smiles at her and reaches out for her phone. "I thought you wouldn't ask."

She watches him dial his number on her phone. He takes out his phone, and she sees her number on the screen. She mutters a quiet thanks when he hands her back her phone. She can't believe that she did something like that.

"Just make sure to call around seven in the evening," he says, not looking up from his phone.

"Why?" She asks.

"I don't want my wife to know."

What? Leanne freezes. Wife? Did she just hear him right? He said wife. Right?

Oh my gosh.

Why the hell didn't she ask if he was married or not? She simply assumed that he was single.

Oh my gosh.

Oh my gosh.

Oh my gosh.

She can feel the panic in her bubbling to the surface. Why didn't she ask? How can she be so stupid?

Vince wants to laugh at her expression when he said that he has a wife but stops when he sees the panic in her eyes. Shit, that joke is out of hand. "Hey," he says. "I was joking. I don't have a wife."

MOTHER OF ALL HOLY. "What the hell?" She screams at him.

Vince can't help and laugh. Leanne stops and watches him laugh. She wants to stay mad at him, but with him laughing like that, she really can't stay mad at him for long. His laughter embraces her. It's genuine laughter and sounds pleasing to her ears. She is used to her fake laughs that she wants to bottle up his genuine laugh and keep it to herself.

"I'm sorry," He says, wiping a tear away. "I'm single, and I assume you are?"

"Yeah."

He smiles at her and waves, heading back towards his car. "I should get going. I'm running late."

She nods. "Sure. I'll see you around …"

"Vince."

"Leanne."

He walks back to his car, smiling. He's already late but it's worth it.

"So…" Anne, her friend, asks her later that night. "What happened after he gave you his number?"

She was on cloud nine when she went home. Her heart was lighter, and her mind was quiet for a while, and she liked it. However, things like those must come with a price, she learned that the hard way.

She glances at the number that he saved on her phone. Vince. The name suits him.

"Lee!" Janine slaps her arm when she didn't respond right away. "What happened next?"

She rolls her eyes at them. "Nothing. He left because he's running late."

A series of displeasure erupts from her three friends. She told them about her encounter with Vince, not everything, she left out the part where Vince found her in a panicked state. If these three find out about that, they will force her to visit Dr. Lynn, and she hates her visits with

Dr. Lynn. Those quizzical eyes of the said doctor unease her. She shudders just thinking about it.

"Where does he work?" Mary asks, looking up from her phone for a split second.

"I don't know."

"What does he do for a living?" Anne asks.

"He's a professor."

"Professor?" Janine says, winking in her direction. "Is this some kind of a Wattpad teacher-student romance?"

Leanne looks at her, horrified. "Dude, I'm twenty-five. I'm far from being a student."

"Technically, we are," Anne points out. "At least for the next three months."

She groans and takes a big bite of her food. "Can we drop it? I'm going to have indigestion if we keep on talking about him."

Mary snorts. "It's not every day that you didn't have an attack when someone tries to talk to you."

"You wouldn't know of it," She murmur under her breath, but she forgot how sharp their sense of hearing is. They put her dead cat to shame.

"What wouldn't we know?" Janine says looking, more like glare at her.

"Uhm ..." She says downing her cold glass of water. She doesn't know how to answer her question. She better answers her question correctly, or they will ship her off to Dr. Lynn, first thing tomorrow. She says in a quiet tone. "Well, I had a mini panic attack."

"What?" The three of them say in chorus.

She slouches at their glare as if to make herself smaller. "I had an attack."

"And why did you leave this out?" Anne asks her with a glare.

She shrugs. "It wasn't that bad."

"It's still an attack!" Mary says, ditching her phone to glare at her. "Why did you keep it from us?"

"We already had this conversation, Lee!" Anne says.

She looks down, feeling guilty for not telling them, but their reaction is the exact reason why she didn't tell them. As much as she loves how caring they are, it's starting to suffocate her. She had a small attack. She always does, that's why it wasn't a big deal to her.

"I know." She sighed. "I just don't want to worry you guys."

"You are making us worry right now."

She sighs. "Vince saw me have an attack."

A series of "What?", "Are you freaking serious?" and "You will visit Dr. Lynn tomorrow" breaks out. The last part didn't dwell on her well. She has no hard feelings, well she does, with Dr. Lynn, she's just uncomfortable with how closed her office is.

"So ..." Janine paused. "Are you going to call him?"

She places her chopsticks beside her bowl. "I don't know. He saw me had an attack and didn't say anything at all."

"How will you know if you won't ask him?" Anne shrugs at her phone.

Leanne sighed, she wants to call him, but there are so many reasons why she shouldn't. To others calling someone is an easy task but to her, it was a battle. Too many what-ifs and questions left answered to the point that it will suffocate her.

"I … I'll figure it out later. He told me to call after seven."

"Why seven?" Mary asks.

Leanne shrugs and continues eating. "He didn't tell."

She doubts that they will understand or find it even funny if she tells them about the joke behind the 7 o'clock.

Vince gets home fifteen minutes to eight. He drops his body on his couch, exhaustion would be the tip of the iceberg. He is too tired to change his clothes, much less cook his dinner, but his growling stomach says otherwise. He regrets not passing by a drive-thru for a burger or a chicken.

He glances at his phone and frowns. Not even a missed call. He hated to admit that he is looking forward to her call. He knows that people in the same situation as her need a little push otherwise, they will stay in their comfort zones. He wants her to make the first move. He had a few speculations on what was going on with her. But he wants it to come from her.

He is a psychology professor in one of the prestigious universities in the country.

He has an assumption of her situation, but something about her intrigued him.

This is stupid, he says to himself. There was no reassurance that she will call just because she asked for his number. He really wants to grab his phone and call her first, but he also wants to see if she will be bold enough to make the first move.

This waiting is driving him insane.

After staring at his phone for five minutes, Vince thought that he is pushing his luck. He heads to the kitchen, finally listening to his grumbling stomach. He frowns when he sees that he doesn't have anything to eat inside his fridge.

I need to go get groceries this weekend, he makes mental note to himself. But he will still forget about it unless he opens his fridge again tomorrow.

He opens his cupboard and praises all the holy, he finds a cup noodle. Not the healthiest, but this will survive him for the night. He pours water into the uncooked noodles and places it in the microwave. He cools it down a bit before diving into it. He let out a satisfied sigh when the heat of the food reaches his stomach. This is heaven.

He let out a burp when he finishes the whole cup, but still no call from her.

I shouldn't have had my hopes up, he says to himself.

"Meow."

He was so engrossed in waiting for her call that he forgot to feed Kutch, his stray cat. The feline glares at him from the couch. Vince chuckles while preparing Kutch's dinner. He watches his cat devour his food.

"Sorry, little guy," he murmurs to his cat.

I shouldn't have expected, he says to himself. With a sigh, he decided to retreat for the night. After one final glance at his phone hoping that she would call, but only to be disappointed.

Leanne wakes up gasping. After three months of restful, uninterrupted sleep, it came back. She runs a hand on her bedridden hair and glances at the time on her phone, sitting on her bedside table. It is only eleven in the evening. She just had fallen asleep. Not a minute later, she wakes up suffocated.

She is alone tonight, just like any other night, because her friends are on the night shift. She has a different schedule from the rest of them, making her alone most of the time, which makes her condition worsen.

She tries to calm herself, but it is of no use. She hates drinking that prescription pill Doctor Lynn gave to her. She hates drinking medicine. Period. So, she had no other choice but to calm herself.

Fuck this life.

Doctor Lynn told her to wrap her arms around herself and tap her shoulders as if someone was hugging her. All the while enumerating all the good things that had happened to her. Thirty minutes had passed, and the voices in her mind won't calm down. She decided to do the calming and grounding technique her father taught her. If it still won't work, then and only then will she drink that horrible medicine.

5 things that you can see.

4 things that you can feel.

3 things that you can hear.

2 things that you can smell.

1 thing that you can taste.

Fucking techniques. None of them works. She reaches for medicine but stops when she sees her phone. Vince. Maybe this is all happening again because of her internal battle into calling him. She tells herself that she will call him at seven, but the clock turned to eight until she had fallen asleep. Not once did she tried to dial his number.

Leanne remembered the feeling of peace when she was talking to him. The voices in her mind ceased their battle just to listen to him.

Every part of her was at peace. She knows and feels that maybe Vince can help her.

With shaky hands, she dials his number. She isn't expecting him to answer the call because of the time, but she held her breath and hoped that he will answer.

"Hello?"

And just like that, the voices quiet down. Her heart is still racing, but it is quiet.

Vince glance at his phone groggily when silence greets him instead. Leanne. She finally called him. He was just about to call it a day when his phone rang. He picked up the call without looking at the screen since he wasn't wearing his glasses. Thinking that it was a colleague calling him, but to his surprise, it was Leanne. But the silence on the other line is deafening.

Maybe she accidentally dials his number? He is about to end the call when he hears her voice. "Vince?"

He let out a sigh that he didn't know that he held. "Leanne?"

"I'm sorry for calling this late."

He frowns at her tone. He sits up and leans on his headboard. "It's okay. Is something wrong?"

"Nothing," he hears her let out a shaky breath. "I just can't sleep."

He frowns at her odd tone. "Are you sure that is the only reason?"

"Yeah." He can hear the lie straight from her tone. "And, also to say that I'm sorry for not calling you earlier."

"This makes up to it anyways."

She scoffs at the other line. "Thank you."

"For what?"

"For answering the call. You don't know how much I needed this."

"Not a problem." He decides not to beat around the bush. "Leanne?"

"Yes?"

"What really happened?"

Silence. Vince thought that she dropped the call when she didn't speak up. "You don't have to say it if it scares you this much."

"How much do you know?" she says breathlessly.

He shrugs but stops when he realized that she couldn't see him. "I have a hunch but ..."

"You wanted me to verify it?"

"Pretty much."

He hears some shuffling in the background before it became quiet again. "What do you know?"

"GAD."

Leanne feels her breath hitch and her palms sweat. He knows. She runs a hand on her forehead, scratching an itch that isn't there. She doesn't know what to say to him. What now? Will his view and opinions about her will change?

"Leanne."

There it is again. The way he speaks her name is different. It has a finality that can make the voices inside of her calm down.

"Yes?" she replies.

"You are doing it again."

She sits up and leans on her headboard. "What do you mean?"

"I know you are having questions right now. You can ask them."

"How ..." She clears her throat when the word came out rougher than usual. "How did you know?"

She hears him sigh. "I'm a psychiatrist."

A strangled cry left her mouth. She has an attraction to the profession that she hated to the core. Of all the profession that is there, why does he have to be a psychiatrist? That is why he knew that she has GAD. He knew from the moment he met her. He *diagnosed* her. Why does he have to be someone she wanted to avoid the most? Why is the world so cruel to her?

"Leanne, breathe."

She didn't know that she was hyperventilating until Vince called her out. She wants to end the call remind her how stupid it was for her to be attracted to him. No matter what he did or how he silenced the voices, he's still a psychiatrist. A fucking psychiatrist.

"Why?" A stupid and dumb question, but her brain isn't functioning properly and just uttered the question that is on her mind.

"Excuse me?"

She rephrases her sentence. "Why didn't you say anything?"

Vince pauses and thinks of the word best to answer her question. He doesn't want to trigger her attacks just because he says the wrong word.

"I didn't want to scare you," he answers quietly.

She scoffs. "Too late for that, don't you think?"

"And I want to get to know you."

Leanne pauses at what he said. He wants to know her. Why? She's not attractive. She doesn't have anything to be proud of. Why would he want to know her?

"Leanne."

There it is again. The peacefulness that follows after he says her name. She used to hate her name; it is too complicated. Nobody can ever spell it right and pronounce it right. It even came to the point that she considered changing her name legally.

"Still there?" Vince's voice pulls her out from her thoughts.

She clears her throat and pulls her mind out of the gutter. "Yeah. I should ... you should go back to sleep. I'm sorry again for calling you this late."

"I'm glad you called," Vince chuckles and runs his hand through his hair. If talking to her can make him this giddy and smiling all by himself, then he's screwed. Big time.

"Me too."

"Lee."

Leanne looks up when she hears her boss call her. She saves the draft report that she made before turning towards her boss. "Yes, boss?"

"Have you given the seminar this Friday a thought?" her boss says. "It's a two-day seminar at a university that the company is hosting."

She frowns. She knows about the seminar that her boss was talking about; it was mailed directly to her. It's a seminar about the proper handling of chemicals and how to read the MSDS. Her boss recommended her as a speaker for the said seminar, but she politely declined the offer. Public speaking wasn't her forte, the thought alone made her want to puke.

"Boss, my answer stays the same." She glances at Kate, her fellow chemist, for help. "Seminars aren't my thing neither is public speaking."

Her boss chuckles. "You won't be giving a lecture anymore. Someone from Material

Analysis will do the lecture instead. You'll be there as a participant."

"Then why should I be there if someone will already do the lecture?" Confusion wrote on her face. "I already know what the topic would be. As much as I want to be free from two days' worth of work, I just think that I will be wasting my time attending the seminar."

"Fine!" her boss concedes. "You'll be giving a lecture. The HR won't agree in removing your name as one of the lecturers since they already submitted the list to the University."

She feels as if a rug has been abruptly removed under her. She can feel her anxiety creep up to her throat, making it hard to breathe. Leanne can hear her boss talk about the topics she will cover for the seminar, but all she can hear are buzzing and loud voices in her head.

She tried to focus her attention on her boss, but the voices in her head were so loud she can't hear anything.

As if sensing her distress her boss says, "I'll send the topics later via mail so you can read on it later."

Leanne didn't feel her boss left his position as she scramble to fix her bearing. She clutches her lab coat when she felt her fingers tremble as her breathing slowly came to normal. It's just a seminar. She'll make small talk and leave. She'll just make sure that she doesn't barf or faint when her anxiety reaches the roof.

"You okay there?" Kate cut off her internal battle. "Thought you went to Mars already."

She scoffs. "I will have if I can."

Kate laughs at her dry humor. "It can't be that bad?"

Leanne glared at her and return to signing sample analysis. "It wasn't funny at all."

The latter shrugs. "Oh, how I wished to see you crawl while you do the lecture."

Friday arrives too soon for Leanne. Clutching her notes, she did one last skimming before the car service provided by the company dropped her and the other person off at the University. It is too late to ask the driver to drive her back to the company. She shouldn't have nudged when her boss bribed her.

A coordinator approaches them and guides them towards the conference hall where the seminar will be held. Leanne is in deep concentration at keeping her anxiety away from the roof that she jumps in shock when someone taps her on her shoulder.

She looks and sees the person she is with gestures to the out-stretch hand before her. She gathered her scattered thoughts and hesitantly shook the person's hand without looking at the face.

"You okay, Leanne?"

Shock, she looks at the person's face and sees Vince. She is shaking his hand without her knowing. Why is he here?

"I'm here for the seminar," Vince answers her thoughts.

Did she say that out loud?

"No." He smiles at her. "Your expression says it all."

After their last conversation, Vince has been stopping by that same Starbucks branch for almost a week in hopes to see her again. On the third day that she doesn't show up, he realizes that it is just a coincidence that Leanne was in the café at that time.

He was looking forward to her calls after the late-night impromptu call, but she never did. It's been a hectic week at the University since a prestigious company will be doing the lecture, and it never crossed his mind to call her again. For him to see her again, unexpectedly, made him want to give a high five to destiny or luck.

"My expression?" Leanne drawls out, still processing the information that Vince is right in front of her. It's been a week since their last conversation, and she isn't expecting him to be present during the seminar.

Vince wants to laugh at her expression only if he isn't in awe of her eyes. They are a bright shade of brown, almost like warm caramel. But the blankness in them made them stand out. How can something so vibrant be so dull at the same time? It amazes Vince.

He is about to answer her, but a fellow professor beats him to it. "Do you know each other?"

"No."

"Yes."

Three pairs of eyes stare at them. The coordinator, his fellow professor, and the other speaker are just listening to the conversation. The two of them have forgotten that there are other people in the hall listening to their conversation.

To ease the sudden tension, the coordinator speaks up. "Professor Elepaño, this is Ms. Argonza and Ms. Austria. They are our speakers for today's seminar."

Austria. Leanne Austria. Vince smile at Leanne. "It's a pleasure to meet you, Ms. Austria, Ms. Argonza."

"Pleasure's all mine," her fellow speaker greets back but she remains frozen, staring at his smile.

It is a smile that can melt the polar caps. A warm embrace of the sun after a storm. It thaws all the voices in her brain, making her think clearly for the first time in two years. Something that her psychiatrist has been trying to cure her off.

Dr. Lynn is going to have a field day when she learns about this.

"Ms. Austria?"

Leanne was so lost in her thoughts that she didn't hear the coordinator call her name. "Yes?" She forces her gaze away from Vince's smile.

"The seminar will start in five minutes," the coordinator points to the chair on the stage, right where everyone can see her. "Once your name is called, you will go up the stage and take the second to the last chair from the podium."

She glances at the chair that the coordinator points out and nod. She can feel her anxiety creep out again as she glances at the chair again. It's so exposed. All eyes will be on her. She feels her heartbeat faster, and her throat clogs up with fear.

What if she messes up? She stutters or utters the wrong word. They will all laugh at her.

"Leanne," Vince calls her name when he sees her pale complexion. "Calm down."

She couldn't hear him. She keeps on glancing at the stage like it was eating her alive.

He gestures to the coordinator to usher their other speaker towards the stage. He has five minutes to calm her down.

"Leanne," he says calmly, reaching to hold her cold hands. "Leanne, listen to me."

She turns towards him. He frowns at how dull her eyes look. He may have her attention, but she is not seeing him. Her beautiful, unique eyes are blank and cold. He rests one hand on her cheek, making her look at *him*.

"Leanne, you can do this," he whispers to her. "You will nail this lecture, and everyone will be listening to you. They will be amazed at how amazing you'll present your lecture. They will applaud you and admire you."

"What-what if ... what if I s-s-tummer?" she murmurs. "T-t-they wi-will laugh at me."

Vince wipes a stray tear that falls on her cheeks and absentmindedly brushes his thumb at the place where the tear fell. "They won't laugh at you."

"How do you know that?"

He smiles at her. "I just do, and I'll be there right behind you."

She looks at him, confused. "Huh?"

He points to the chair beside hers. "I'll be sitting right there since I'll be saying the closing remarks."

Leanne doesn't know how Vince did it, but he calmed her down. Maybe it was the thought that he'll be beside her throughout the seminar or the soothing motion of his thumb at her cheeks that put her to ease. She's able to breathe properly again. Her heart rate's back to normal, and she can feel Vince's warmth from his hand that is resting on her cheeks.

Leanne takes a deep breath, and the sweet minty scent of Vince invades her system and makes her completely at ease.

"Ready to blow their minds?"

She takes one more sniff of his scent before nodding, and with the most confident posture that she can muster, she says, "I'm ready."

Leanne let out a sigh of relief when they are finally ushering out of the conference hall. She doesn't expect that she will be doing a lecture without stuttering, and everyone was actively listening and participating when she did a Q & A after her lecture.

"Great job," the coordinator says, shaking their hands before heading back to the hall, leaving her and the other lecturer. He spots where the company car left her this morning.

Leanne glances at her certificate and souvenir before giving herself a pat on the back for a job well done.

"Are you going to wait for the company car?"

She removes her gaze at her souvenir and turns to her fellow lecturer. Was her name Sheila or Sandy? She can't remember.

"Uh …" she trails off and digs for her phone. She forgets that she should call her boss for the company car to fetch them.

Sheila or Sandy holds up her hand. "I won't be riding back with you. My husband is going to fetch me."

Leanne stops in the middle of searching for her boss' contact number. "Uh … sure?"

A gray Honda Civic stops in front of them, and Sheila or Sandy waves at her before hopping inside the car, leaving her staring at the taillight of the disappearing car.

What …?

She let out a sigh. She doesn't want to bother the company car to fetch her alone, and she's done for the day anyway. Her ringtone snaps her to reality. Speaking of the devil.

"Boss?"

"How's the lecture?"

She shrugs before realizing that her boss can't see her. "It actually went well."

"See?" She can hear him smile. "It wasn't so bad, isn't it?"

It was bad, she wants to say, but keep it to herself. "Not half bad."

"Did you call the company car to fetch you?"

"There's no need, boss." She tucks her souvenir and certificate under her pits as she single-handedly opens her bag. "I'll be heading home anyway. There is no need to bother."

"How about the other lecturer?"

"Her husband fetched her."

She let out a sigh of relief when she successfully unzips her bag. She sandwiches her phone between her ear and shoulder as she fixes her things so that the certificate won't crumple.

"Are you sure?"

She fixes herself before answering. "I'm sure."

"Alright then, get home safely."

"Thanks," she says before ending the call.

She sighs and glances around the area. All she needs to do is find the exit. She is so engrossed in reading her notes en route to the university that she didn't pay attention to the direction that the car takes. Now she regrets not calling the company car.

She's about to turn when her phone chimes for an incoming message.

Psychiatrist: Have you left the Uni?

Leanne frowns at her phone. Psychiatrist? Why will Dr. Lynn ask her if she left the university? Oh. Right, Vince.

Leanne: Not yet. Y?

She quickly renames Vince's contact in her phone. It might cause question to others who will see her phone, or she'll confuse Vince to Dr. Lynn and will never pick up the call.

Vince: Wait for me.

Leanne: ok.

Vince chuckles at her replies. He quickly fixes his things before saying his goodbyes to his colleagues. He doesn't have to search for her since her red tips are the first thing he sees when he opens the door of the conference hall.

He was—is proud of her. Everyone was in awe at her during the lecture. Everyone was seeing what he was seeing at that time. A beautiful, confident woman. She captured everyone's attention during the lecture.

Everyone was listening to her and even participate in the ice breaker challenge that she did on the spot.

Vince thought that he had read her, but he was wrong beyond many levels. He wants to know more about her, beyond the rough and fragile exterior that she built around her.

"Hey." He captures her attention when he stands beside her. "Congratulations on not vomiting back there."

"Thank you." She gives him a tight-lipped smile. Her brown eyes remain indifferent, and it irritates him. He stops himself from frowning.

"Are you heading somewhere?"

She shakes her head, and he is mesmerized at the flowing motion of the red tips of her hair. Everything she does makes him stop and want to capture it.

"I'm going to head home, but I don't know where the way out is," she frowns at her surroundings.

Unconsciously, he reaches up and soothes the wrinkled skin between her eyebrows. The small gesture made Leanne stop. It was that feeling again. A sense of tranquility. She often read in books that they feel butterflies or that their heart beats faster whenever they see their special someone. Leanne never felt that way towards Vince.

There are no butterflies or horses in her stomach, no twitchy sweaty palms or heartbeats that can be heard with how hard it is palpitating. She never felt any of those when she met Vince for the first time, and it bothers her. What she's feeling wasn't written in any romance books that she read. It was something that she wasn't prepared for, and she hate the feeling of getting off guard.

"Would like you like to join me for a cup of coffee?"

Vince's voice brings her out of her reverie. She clears her throat before answering him. "I already had a cup this morning."

She notices his smile falters a bit, and it brings uncomfortable feelings in her. She quickly retrieves her words and changes them. "But I'm fine with fruit tea or milk tea."

He let out a chuckle, and she taps herself mentally for a job well done. She can feel a smile edging out to break from her face, but she scolds herself and remain indifferent. His smile, laugh, and chuckles are infectious. It makes her want to smile with him and enjoy a simple joke.

"Well ..." Vince drawl out. "I don't want you to change your mind again. Shall we?"

She nods and follows Vince towards the parking lot in front of the conference hall. She watches him walk towards a red MG 5 and open the door for her before walking towards the driver's seat. She hates to admit that the simple gesture he displayed warmed her panicking heart.

"Seat belt."

She quickly complies and takes a deep breath. The inside of the car smells entirely of lemon and a little bit of mint, an unmanly scent that fits him perfectly. She subtly watches him as he drives towards their destination, and she let out a quiet gasp when he parks outside of Starbucks where they first met.

"I hope this café is okay with you," Vince glance at her before killing the engine.

She nods and moves to open the door, but Vince grabs her arm to stop her. The simple contact made her pause. She stares at the hand that is still on her arm. It's warm in contrast to her cold ones. She sighs when the warmth spread throughout her entire body. For years, she thought she might never feel this kind of contentment. Something so common but rare for her.

Vince study her face. Despite the indifferent face that she's holding, her eyes were very expressive, and he absorb everything. Shock. Awe. Contentment. In a matter of seconds, her eyes flashed with those three emotions. He wants her to open up to him but forcing her will only make her run away from him.

A tear drops from her face, and with his free hand he reaches up to wipe it off. The moment his thumb came in contact with her skin, she flinches, and her eyes met his. They are back to being cold and guarded.

Leanne didn't know that she was crying until Vince wipes her tears away from her. She unconsciously flinches at the sudden action but didn't make any move to remove his fingers away from her face. She remains impassive as he wipes her tears away. He has the most expressive face and eyes that she has ever known.

They express what he feels. She can see that her tears and actions bothered him. If only she was strong enough to tell him everything. If only she's not a broken fragment of herself, then maybe, just maybe she can be worth it for him.

"What are you thinking?" Vince whisper, afraid that if he talks loudly, she will wither away from him. He likes the small tranquility they currently have.

She opens her mouth to answer him, but nothing came out. She has so many things to tell him, so many thoughts to share. But her voice box refuses to cooperate with her, and it made her so frustrated with herself.

"Why are you hiding, Leanne?"

She stares at him in shock. No one, *no one,* not even Dr. Lynn asks her that specific question. Four words and she has completely swept off her bearings. She doesn't know how to answer him. How to lie to him since he asked a question no one ever bothered to ask her.

"What ... what do you mean?" She croaks out, building her walls tighter than they usually are. "I'm ... I'm not hiding anything."

Vince frowns at her lie and decides to drop it. He can't help the feeling of disappointment at her dismissal, but he schools his expression before straightening himself. He coughs the clog from his throat. "We better head inside if we don't want to miss their limited-edition buns."

Vince thought that he was able to hide it, but Leanne saw it all.

It's been two days since their coffee date, and Leanne's contemplating picking up her phone and calling Vince. She looks at her phone like it is about to eat her out. It's her rest day, and all she did was chicken out every time she presses on Vince's contact.

She drops her body at her bed with a sigh and stares at the ceiling. She wants to talk to him just to talk about anything. Heck, they'll even talk about the weather if they wanted to.

Leanne reaches up and traces the place where Vince's thumb brushes her tears away. It's been days since then, but she can still feel the soft brush of his fingers on her cheeks. After the episode inside Vince's car, she expected the atmosphere would be awkward and heavy, but Vince proved her wrong. They talked about anything except her GAD.

Vince knew what questions to ask to maintain the conversation flowing. He knew what topic would drain her and what topic she was most interested in, and even after two hours, she still wanted more. He has this certain charm that will make you stop and listen to him regardless of the topic.

She likes the way his eyes lit up when he talks about something he's interested in. The way his lips quirk up with his corny jokes and the way he makes hand gestures, especially when he wants to make a point, or the way his brows furrow when he's disagreeing with something. Leanne noticed those small details about him during their coffee date.

Was it a date?

Vince asked her for a coffee. So, it may be a coffee date.

But was it a date?

Leanne rolls to her front and groans out her frustration on her pillow. This is stressing her out. She decides on giving up when her phone rings. She quickly picks up her phone and answer without bothering to check the caller.

"Hello?" she answers in a cheerful voice. She made it so obvious that she was waiting for his call. She composes herself and tries again. "Hello?"

"That's odd." Dr. Lynn's voice reaches her.

She pauses and glances at the caller's name to see Dr. Lynn's contact instead of Vince. She sighs and rubs her neck. Speaking of the devil.

"Hello, Dr. Lynn," she murmurs. Her excitement vanishes and is replaced with a cold blanket that she was used to. She winces at feeling the sensation again. She got a little taste of warmth that she forgot what the cold felt like.

"You seemed excited a while ago. Were you waiting for someone?"

Yes, she wants to say but she opted to lie to promptly end the conversation. "No."

Dr. Lynn sigh on the other line. "Leanne..."

There it is. The sense of disappointment. She can't seem to run away from that feeling. She remains quiet, waiting until Dr. Lynn decided to break the silence.

"Did you take any of the medications that I prescribe to you?"

She gulps and stares at the ceiling. She can tell the truth and be scheduled for an appointment right away or lie and not see Dr. Lynn until the next few months. "For this week? I haven't."

"You know, what I'm talking about Leanne."

She pulls open her bedside drawer and notice that there isn't any tablet missing. She hasn't taken anything. She let out a sigh of relief and answer Dr. Lynn. "I haven't taken anything."

"Oh?" She can hear the surprise in her doctor's tone. "That is great progress, Leanne. Keep it up, and you'll be done with me in no time."

She plans to. She didn't bother in saying her goodbyes and quickly drop the phone call. She glances at the drawer again and frowns. Does Vince have something to do with this? She usually takes one table per month, sometimes more depending on the situation or how severe her episodes are. But ever since she met Vince, not once did it cross her mind to intake one.

Wanting to prove something, she dials Vince's number. She places it on speakerphone before dropping it beside her. One ring. Two rings. Three rings. The next one would be voicemail.

"Hello?"

She yelps in surprise, not expecting him to pick up. She places a hand on her chest to calm her palpitating heart.

"Leanne?" Vince glanced at his phone just to make sure that Leanne didn't end the call when she doesn't reply right away.

"Hey." She sighs in relief.

Vince stops checking his students' research papers and focuses on her tone. It is the only way for him to know what she's feeling right now. "What happened?"

She should lie. But before she can figure out a lie, her mouth beats her to it. "Mm ... my psychiatrist called."

"And then?" He fidgets, anxious in his chair at what she's going to say next. He admires her honesty for answering him truthfully, but mostly he is flattered that she called him when she's feeling upset.

She is quiet for a few seconds contemplating telling him about her condition before answering. There are some things that he shouldn't know. Vince knew about her GAD, that's it. He doesn't know that she's taking any medications to relieve her anxiety. "She asked me if I have taken any of her prescriptions."

Vince is taken back by what she said. He doesn't know that her GAD is this severe. All this time, he assumed that she was at the stage where she's only undergoing group therapies and sessions. He can visualize her, slouching at her bed with all the burden that she's carrying. He wants to help her carry her burden, but that is a decision that she has to make on her own.

He wants to hug her.

He wants to console her.

He wants to tell her that it will be okay.

But those aren't what she needs right now. Words of comfort aren't what she needs right now. She wants someone to listen to her, and that's what he will be doing.

"Did you take the prescriptions?" he asks tentatively while crossing his fingers.

"No, I haven't."

"That's—"

"I haven't taken anything since I met you."

A wide grin covers his face at her confession. He runs a hand at his mouth to feel the smile on his face. He never felt this light, elated, and every other synonym there is that is related to happiness. Not even when he graduated and earned his degree. The sense of accomplishment that he feels with her statement is beyond his capability.

This woman will be the death of him, Vince claps himself. "I'm flattered, sweetheart."

Leanne pauses and places a hand over her heart to feel it beating calmly despite his endearment to her. She likes it. She's not a fan of endearments, but she likes the way he calls her sweetheart. Like actually mean it. She covers her mouth to refrain herself from squealing from the euphoric feeling that she is in.

"I like it," she says before she can stop herself.

"What did you like, sweetheart?" There it is again.

She can feel herself burn with embarrassment. Thank heavens he can't see her. Otherwise, he's going to see red from the tips of her toes to her hair. She let out a deep breath to calm herself. She's acting like a teenager talking to her crush for the first time.

"Leanne? Sweetheart?"

She smiles while staring at her wall. She's so far gone. "I like it when you call me sweetheart."

"Really?" Vince let out a low chuckle. "Never knew you are into endearments."

"I'm not, but it feels different when you say it."

Vince leans back on his chair with a silly smile on his face. The words accidentally slipped from his mouth, and he tried saying it again. The words taste familiar like he's been calling her that all their lives. He was expecting an opposite reaction than what he expected from her.

"What if I said babe instead of sweetheart?"

Leanne shudders in disgust. "Don't ever call me that. Babe is a pig in the city."

He laughs at her reference. "How about baby?"

"Do I look like a newborn baby to you?"

Vince can't help but laugh at her questions. He can't help but tease her a little bit more. "I can call you darling."

She rolls her eyes, but the smile on her face never left. "My grandma probably called my grandpa that."

"Do you really have to comment on everything?" he says in an exasperated tone.

Leanne laughs at his exasperation. She's been controlling her laughter until he is so close to pissing off that she had enough. It feels good to laugh genuinely. The one that can make your stomach hurt and roll on the floor for laughing. She got so used to her fake laughs that she forgot what she sounds like if she laughs genuinely. When was the last time that she was able to laugh like this?

It's because of Vince. Ever since she met him, she can see changes in herself that her psychiatrist wasn't able to do in the three years she's been in therapy. In a month, she's able to quiet down the voices in her head. She was able to laugh until her stomach hurts, and for the first time in her life, she wanted to get better. She wanted to be able to stand by and be with Vince without her demons hunting her.

She wanted to remember who she was like. The woman who laughs without inhibitions. The woman who has goals and dreams. The strong, bright, and friendly woman she used to be.

"It's good to hear you laugh," Vince says but frowns when he heard her laughter turn into tears. "Sweetheart?"

"I'm fine." She sniffs and chuckles at the same time like a maniac. "I'm actually fine. I'm just … happy. Really happy."

Vince leans forwards in his seat when he suddenly has the urge to hug her. He clenches his hand when he heard her sniff. "Why are you happy, Sweetheart?"

Leanne smiles at the wall. "You made me laugh, Vince." She let out a sigh. "It feels good to laugh again."

Why? It was at the tip of Vince's tongue to ask her, but he held back. He wants to know everything there is about her, but he's willing to wait for her to willingly open up to him. Pushing her would only compel her to stay away from him, and the thought of her ignoring and staying away from him made him unease.

"Are you available tomorrow?" he asks instead.

"Yeah, why?"

"I want to take you somewhere."

Leanne glances at her phone as if Vince is sitting beside her and she's trying to understand him. She's trying not to read between the lines and keep her hopes up. "Where?"

"That's for me to know and for you to find out."

Leanne pauses. What should she say? She racks up her brain for any stored smart comeback but found nothing. She mentally slaps herself for being allergic on the subject of flirting. She could use a trick or two. Before she can humiliate herself, Vince spoke up to her relief.

"Is seven good with you?"

She frowns and removes her phone from a loudspeaker. "It's too early, don't you think?"

Warmth seeped through her being when he chuckled. "In the evening."

"Oh," she paused, pretending to think. "Seven is okay."

"Good," Vince smiles and wince when he sees his chaotic stack of papers. "See you tomorrow?"

She hums in agreement before ending the call without waiting for his goodbye. Vince gape at his phone when she abruptly drops the call while Leanne glowers at her thumb for pressing the end button first out of habit.

To avoid seeming like a bitch, she quickly composes a message to Vince.

Leanne: I'm sorry for cutting you off.

Vince read her message and sigh. Her anxiety is taking off again.

Vince: It's alright. You don't have to be sorry.

She didn't know that she held her breath until she let out a sigh of relief. She's about to reply when her phone chimes again.

Vince: Get some rest, sweetheart. Rest that loud mind of yours.

Leanne: okay.

Vince chuckle at her reply. She always has to be the last say. He places his phone on his table and glance at the invitation he threw at the trash bin beside his table.

Will she be okay about this?

It was December 27, two days after Christmas.

Leanne was in her second year in college when it happened, but it was only until she was twenty-one when it triggered.

She grew up thinking that it was normal. That all other kids experience it like her.

It got worst as she grew up. It was strangling her, drowning her.

She always tries to claw her way out of it, but its hold on her just tighten.

She can't breathe.

Help, she screams. Help.

Somebody, help.

Leanne gasps and clutch her throat the moment she wakes up. She tries to calm her labored breathing with the exercises Dr. Lynn gave to her, but she keeps on remembering the hand that was clutching her throat. It was the same dream every damn night.

She run a shaky hand on her sweaty forehead and shivered when her cold hands touched her skin. This is so fucked up.

She automatically reaches for her medicine drawer but stops before she can take out the bottle.

Does she really need this? Yes.

She can just call Vince and ask for help. He's still asleep. Don't bother him with your problems.

How about Dr. Lynn? She'll tell you to drink the medicine.

In times like this, she hates being alone. She thinks about everything if she's alone.

Thoughts that she has no control of. Voices that talk all at once make her want to bash her head into a wall to silence them. She feels that she's drowning again.

She cries while clutching her medicine bottle. She wants to drink a pill to silence everything, but the thought of Vince knowing that she intake one makes her stop and hesitate. What's happening to her? She never hesitates in intaking a pill, especially at times like this. At times where her nightmares seem to follow her even when she's awake.

She howls as the voices get louder as every second passes that she hesitates. She just wanted to rest.

She's tired.

One pill won't hurt.

She doesn't have to tell him.

Unable to resist the yearning for rest, she shakily opens the bottle and takes one pill. She quickly drowns it out with the water that she left on her bedside table before she can change her mind. She nimbly places the bottle back into the drawer before laying on her back.

She sighs when she felt her chest lighten and the unknown hand from her throat disappear. She stares at the wall as the voices slowly disappear. Her heartbeats return to normal, and her body isn't shaking like it was a few minutes ago.

She covers her eyes with her arm when her body finally calmed down. She thought she was getting better. She hasn't had that dream for a week and hasn't heard the voices for almost a month. What changed?

She moves to pick up her phone to cancel her plans with Vince, but her phone fell on the floor as she grabs it. Her arm is so weak that she didn't attempt to move it anymore. She closes her eyes and let sleep swallow her.

Leanne wakes up hours later to a splitting headache, sore body, and rough throat. She weakly pulls herself up and heads to the bathroom to do her necessities. She's on her way to the kitchen when she sees Anne walking towards the bathroom.

"Morning," she says hoarsely. Water.

She let out a pained cough when her dry voice box rubs along her throat. Anne frowns at her friend as she watches Leanne rub her aching throat.

"You okay?" she asks, bothered at her friend's pale face.

Leanne nods and head to the kitchen to grab room temperature water. She gulps the whole cup and sighs when the roughness in her throat disappears. She takes another cup for her thirst.

"Lee."

She turns to see Anne still standing in front of the bathroom, staring at her worriedly. "Yeah?"

"Are you okay?"

She nods. "Yeah. Why are you asking?"

"You didn't intake any pill, right?"

She pauses for a split second while she was taking out a leftover baguette from the fridge. She can feel Anne's eyes on her as she moves around the kitchen. "I didn't intake anything at all, Anne," she lies.

Anne remains quiet while she surveys her friend's actions. Leanne just lied to her. She notices how Leanne won't look at her while saying that she didn't intake the pill Dr. Lynn prescribed her. Instead of pushing her, Anne left her alone in the kitchen.

Leanne let out a sigh of relief when she felt Anne's stare leave her back. She holds on to the kitchen counter and let out a deep breath. This is why she hates taking those pills. They make her more worn out than she used to. She looks at the baguette that is left untouched. It suddenly doesn't look so appetizing.

She returns the baguette to the fridge and fills her water bottle before heading to her room. She sees her phone on the floor beside her bed and realizes that she has plans with Vince that day. She grabs her phone and checks if there are any cracks on the screen.

She groans when she notices the time. She only has an hour to get ready. She didn't have the urge to go out right now. She doesn't feel like walking, eating, or even smiling. She knew that if she pushes herself this evening, she might snap at Vince or not appreciate Vince's effort at all, and it will be unfair on Vince's part.

Without further ado, she dials Vince's number.

"Sweetheart?" Vince had just gotten out of the shower when he heard his phone ring. Seeing that it was Leanne on his phone screen he immediately answers.

"Umm … Vince?"

He frowns when he noticed how hoarse her voice is. "Yeah?"

"Is it okay if we do a raincheck for today? I'm going down with the flu and—"

"It's fine," he cut her off. He is a bit disappointed that she canceled last minute, but if she's not feeling well, it's better to let her rest than strain her health.

Leanne felt bad for lying to him and for not telling him about her pill intake. He was elated when he found out that she hasn't taken a pill. She rubs the spot where her heart is when she felt a slight discomfort at disappointing him.

"Are you sure?" She clears her throat when it is starting to sound hoarse again.

"I'm sure, Sweetheart." He runs a hand through his wet hair. "How are you feeling?"

"Like shit," she tells him honestly. Sweetheart. He calls her sweetheart, but she doesn't deserve that endearment today.

"Have you taken any medicines?"

She half-lied. "I did."

"Why don't you get a quick nap?" Vince says, grabbing sweatpants. He's starting to feel cold since he's only wrapped in towels.

Leanne bit her lip to stop herself from crying. She hates this claustrophobic sensation that she's feeling right now. She's used to lying to everyone about anything, but this is her first time feeling guilty for lying. She clears her throat to remove the tears that are clogging in her eyes.

She doesn't want to be alone tonight. She's too scared to fall asleep. What if she gets those dreams again? She can't afford to take a second pill.

"Doyouthinkyoucancomeover?"

"What?" Vince pauses in searching for a shirt when she mumbles her words. "Might want to slow down, Sweetheart."

She sighs and closes her eyes to hide her from the embarrassment she gave to herself. Sweetheart. "Can you come over? I don't want to be alone."

Vince halts whatever he was doing and just slowly processes her words. He blinks once, twice before her question sinks in. "Are you sure?"

"Yes." She rolls to her side. Her phone pressed between her ear and her pillow. "Please?"

He sighs and runs his hand through his hair. He can't resist her now that she said please.

He also noticed something in her tone that made him want to see her.

"I'll be there."

Vince calms himself as he drives his way towards Leanne's apartment. Right after she narrated her address to him, he quickly ends the call and headed to his car. It was a miracle that no enforcement stopped him from exceeding the speed limit. He turns towards her street and park right in front of their apartment door.

He promptly places his car in park and heads to the door. He's about to press on the doorbell when the door suddenly opens. Three women were staring at him, and he realizes that he was blocking the doorway. He moves to the side and presses the doorbell but stops when one of the women speaks up.

"The doorbells are not working," she says, gesturing to the buttons. "They are mostly for display."

"Oh," he says. "Thank you for telling me."

She nods, her bleached hair bobbing. "Also, use the stairs. The elevator is currently under maintenance."

"Thank you again."

Before the group left, he calls their attention. "Which floor is Unit 2-A?"

The three women questioning gazes land on him. The one with brown hair says, "Why are you asking about our unit floor?"

Their unit? This must be Leanne's roommates. He composes himself since first impression matters. "I'm Vince, Leanne's—"

"You're Vince?" the tallest woman asks him. "The psychiatrist Vince?"

He was shocked with her statement would be an understatement. He quickly composes himself with her question. Leanne probably told them about him. That's the most logical explanation. "Yeah, that's me. Is Leanne in your apartment?"

"She is," the blonde says. "She's coming down with flu or something."

Vince glance at the door, surreptitiously hoping to hide his agitation. He wants to go upstairs already, but he doesn't want to come as rude in front of her friends. He needs their approval if he wants to pursue her. Janine notices his impatience when he glances at the open door for the second time around.

"The first door you see when you reached the second floor," she says to remove his unease.

He gives her a thankful smile, and as if his butt is on fire, dash towards their apartment. The three of them glance at one another before giggling. Oh, their friend is one lucky girl.

Leanne wakes up with a start when she heard her phone ring. She blindly pats the space beside her until she feels the vibrating rectangle device. She again answers it without looking at her screen.

"Hello?" she grumbles, burrowing her face deeper in her pillow.

"Sweetheart? Might want to open your door?"

Leanne sits up so suddenly that she momentarily pauses when her vision blackens, and she is hit with a wave of dizziness from the sudden movement. When she gets her bearing straighten up, she leaves her bed and head to the front door. What she sees made her pause and take a deep breath.

Vince is standing outside her door, one hand in his sweatpants' pocket while the other is holding the phone to his ear. He is wearing a black shirt that is not too tight or too loose. Vince doesn't have a toned muscle like those in the magazines or billboards, but she knows that he goes to the gym every once in a while, just to maintain his figure. He is wearing an eyeglass, and this is the first time that Leanne sees him wearing one. His glasses enhance his brown eyes, making them pop out more.

The latter smiles when he notices that she is checking him out. He drops the call and lets himself be under her scrutiny. He also can't help but roam his gaze at her. She's wearing a matching silk pajama. Some of her hair strands cover her face and as if he's doing it all his life reaches up to move those strands aside.

Leanne gasped when she felt Vince's touch on her face. She snaps back to reality and realizes how close they are to one another. She can feel his breath on her face. The scent of mint invades her senses, making her disorganized mild calm down. She thought all it takes was his voice to calm her. Everything about him calms her, his scent, his voice, his smile, and just him.

"Hi."

She holds back the smile that almost got out. She lets out a breathless reply. "Hi."

"I met your friends' downstairs."

She looks at him in shock. Oh, shit. "Really? Did they say something to you?"

He shrugs. "I just found out that you gossip me to your friends."

She snorts and feels a slight tilt of her mouth. "I need their opinion about something."

Vince is awestruck with her smirk. It's not a smile, but it is the closest thing to smiling. He made sure to capture it and store the memory somewhere in the back of his mind. "About what?"

She shrugs and didn't answer him. "Want to come in?"

Vince nods and follows her towards her apartment. He takes a quick survey of the room and notices a disorderly stack of books in one corner, a small aquarium an arms width away from the books, a four cube DIY closet pushed at the very corner, and a solid wood cabinet adjacent to the door. Aside from those things the room is bare.

"Please leave your shoes by the rack over there," she says after she closes the door behind him. "I just vacuumed and swept the whole apartment.

He follows her instruction and heads further into the room.

"Sorry about the mess," Leanne says, folding the laptop tables and leaning them at a wall. "We weren't expecting a guest."

He waves her worries away. "It's much tidier than mine."

She rolls her eyes at his statement and continues to put her scattered books into the pile. "Have you eaten dinner? I can make something if you are willing to wait."

He frowns at her statement. She's supposed to be resting because she's sick and not fussing over him. "Aren't you supposed to be resting?"

She shot him a contemptuous look. "I was. I've been asleep the whole day. I need to move around or do something because laying in the bed is making me sicker."

"Okay," he then sighs in defeat. "Let me cook you something while you arrange some stuff."

"No," She glares at him while holding a bean bag. "I canceled our plans, and making a meal is the least that I can do."

"You are sick, and it is normal to cancel, especially if you are sick. I'm not an asshole, Leanne."

She pauses at whatever she was doing when Vince calls her by her name. It sounded weird when he calls her name. She got used to him calling her sweetheart these past few days. "Fine."

Vince hid his smile when he sees her frown at him. "What would you like to eat?"

She shrugs. "Surprise me, I guess?"

He nods and heads in the direction of the kitchen. Leanne silently scoffs when she saw the smug look that was on his face when she conceded. This will be the first and last time that she's going to concede. She continues to arrange some of their stuff when she heard the sizzle of the pan, and on cue, her stomach growled. She hasn't eaten anything yet.

She hurriedly finishes her business in the living room before heading to the kitchen. If only drooling isn't disgusting that would probably be what she's doing right now. Vince looks at ease and home in her personal space. He moves gracefully while stirring something in the pan.

She can't help but admire his muscles that are flexing while he is tossing the ingredients into the pan.

Damn, how did she get so lucky?

She hasn't told him.

That thought made her frown all of the sudden. When she opened the door to Vince a while ago the thoughts about her drinking the pills and her dreams disappear. She got distracted with Vince and his sweatpants that she forgot about her hysteria yesterday.

"Is stir fried okay with you?"

Vince's voice brought her back. She looks in his direction and sees him looking at her, holding a pan filled with vegetables and noodles. She then realizes that he was waiting for her answer.

"Yes." She smiles at him. "It's fine with me."

Her smile slowly disappears when she sees that Vince is gaping at her. It then dawned on her that she smiled at him. He had heard her laugh on the phone, but he has never seen her smile, and Vince was caught off guard at how vibrant she was when she smiled. Her lips stretch wide to reach her ear, and the edges of her eyes wrinkle at the movement.

He tightens his hold on the pan when he felt it nearly slip from his fingers and immediately fixes himself when he sees Leanne going back to her shell upon realizing that she smiled at him.

No.

Not yet.

A few seconds more.

It was gone as fast as it came, and Vince can't help feeling a little downcast when her smile vanished. But something is better than nothing. He heard her laugh one time, and then, he saw her smile, small steps.

As if sensing that she's about to hyperventilate, Vince speaks up. "I knew a smile would look pretty on you, Sweetheart."

Before her mind wanders to places, Vince's tone made her look at him. She knew that she has a panic look on her face, and for once, she didn't hide it from him. She's surprised to see Vince smiling at her, but upon seeing her panicked face, he closed the distance between them and pull her into a hug.

The moment Vince's arms wrapped around her; she forgot the reason why she was panicking. She forgot everything, and all her senses focused on the warmth that his body is giving her cold hollow heart. She can feel her heart beating steadily, and for the first time in her life, everything suddenly brightens.

His scent calms her.

His warmth melts her.

His kindness reaches her.

She's falling for him.

And it scares her more than her demons.

"Um…" Vince lets go of her and scratch his nape in embarrassment. He shouldn't have hugged her, but the urge to wrap his arm around her was so strong that his body moved on its own. He should have asked for her permission before hugging her. What if she hates it? "I'm sorry. I shouldn't have hugged you without asking."

She looks at him, and Vince can't help but squirm in uncertainty. He can't read her expression, and what she did next surprises him. She made the move to hug him. She presses herself to his body and sighs. A sigh of relief. Like he lifted all of her worries away.

He returns her hug. She smells a bit of lavender and something else that he can't point out. He places his chin on top of her head to hide his smile. Vince can't help but feel a little giddy. If Leanne wasn't hugging him, he would have made punches in the air from joy.

Leanne bit the inside of her cheek to stop her lips from smiling when she felt Vince sway their bodies from side to side gently. He's rocking her, and she likes it. The smile that she's trying to hide broke out when she felt Vince place his chin on top of her head. She burrows her face deeper into his chest and inhales his minty scent.

How long will this happiness last? How long will everything be fine?

She doesn't know. As much as she wants to cherish the moment, the unspecified events scare her. The things that she doesn't have control of scare her. She always makes sure that she has everything in order. She lived her life in an orderly, predictable manner because it was the only thing in her life that she can control.

But Vince came, and she felt like she was losing control of her emotions. She's feeling things that aren't in her comfort zone, feelings that she doesn't know how to approach because she's not familiar with them. Safe? Ease? Contentment? Love? She's not sure. She knows that what she's feeling for Vince is deeper than a simple infatuation.

Her thoughts cease when her stomach decided to make itself known. She closes her eyes praying that Vince didn't hear it, but when she feels and hears a rumble coming from him, she knows that he heard her stomach.

"Would you mind eating a cold noodle?" She mumbles against his body.

She feels him shaking his head before removing his arms around her. She let out a disappointed sigh and reluctantly removed her arms around him. "I'll reheat the noodle."

Before she can move away from him, he grabs her hand made her look at him. Leanne stand transfixed at his smile. It makes her feel sunshine and rainbows.

"Thank you," he says, reaching up to cup her face.

"What for?" she whispers as she feels her voice not cooperating with her because her mind is short-circuited by his touch.

"For smiling."

She feels her breath hitch with what he said. She doesn't know how to answer him. Should she say thank you? Nobody thanks anybody for smiling. Vince did. She studies him and sees him smiling at her genuinely.

"Why did you thank me?" She can't help but ask.

He shrugs, turning to reheat the noodles. "It's the first time I saw you smile. I can't help but feel a bit sense of achievement."

She can feel her face heat up with his words. Thankfully he has his back to her. Otherwise, he'll see another first from her. She hasn't known him that long, but she has experienced many first with him. She should be scared worried about the way she's acting but opening up to him slowly feels right. He doesn't push her. He let her slowly show herself to him. But how long? How long will he stay before he gets tired of waiting for her?

"Knock. Knock."

She looks at him and see a worried look pass him. "Penny for your thoughts?"

Leanne subtly shook her head at him before sending him a tight-lipped smile, dismissing him. He watches her grab the plates and other cutlery and place it on the table. Her expression bothered him, especially after he thanked her. There was an unknown expression on her face like she was debating whether to accept his thanks or not and how to answer his question.

While waiting for the microwave to be done reheating the noodles, he silently observes her from his peripheral. He noticed that her steps are quiet and light. She's barefoot, but he can't hear a single tap of her feet on the floor. It was like she was afraid to disturb someone by making a sound. He's fixated on her movements. The way she fixes the table setting for the two of them. From the plates down to the cups, everything was in order.

Vince frowns as he continues to watch her. He wants to know what happened to her. What pushed her GAD? He cast the thoughts aside and continue to appreciate her. He notices that the red tips of her hair are being accentuated by her bun. It was the first thing he noticed from her, and he can't help but smile at how they met. Who would have thought?

"Why are you looking at me like that?"

Vince cut off his thoughts when he heard her voice. "Like what?"

"Like I'm something special."

"You are, Sweetheart."

Her breath hitched. She doesn't know how to reply to him. A big part of her wanted to turn around and pretend that she hasn't heard him, but she also wanted to try things out with Vince without being scared of what the future might come. To do that, she has to start changing her interaction with him. Baby steps.

So, instead of answering him or contradicting his statement, she smiles at him. A genuine smile. Not the tight-lipped smirk that she would always show other people but a full-blown genuine smile that shows her teeth. She can feel the smile reach her ears, but she didn't hold back like she used to. For once, she acknowledges and embraces the giddy feeling Vince is giving her.

Vince pauses when he sees her smile. He wants to close the distance between them and kiss the smile on her face. He wanted to know what her smile tastes like. He had previous relationships, but no one gave him the urge to kiss someone so badly as he does with Leanne.

But the thought of her sharing that smile with others sour his mood, and Leanne seeing the shift in his expression made her smile falter a bit. "What's wrong?"

He shook his head and grab the noodles from the microwave. Before Leanne can warn him, Vince grabs the hot bowl with his bare hands, and he yelps from the sting. His mood darkens when he drops the noodles that Leanne made for them. Just great.

"Oh my gosh, Vince!" Leanne dashes to his side and grabs his hand to inspect the burn.

She quickly drags his hand under running water before heading to her room to grab an Aloe Vera gel. She pauses on her way to the kitchen when she sees Vince glare at his fingers. She walks towards him warily, afraid to disturb his thought.

"Vince?"

She sees him slightly flinch upon hearing her voice. He removes his hand under the water and closes the faucet off. He wipes his wet hand on his sweatpants before facing her. She can see him try to hide his emotions. She can't read a person's emotions unless they told her so, but with Vince, she quickly knows what he's feeling, and being indifferent and emotionless bothers her. It didn't sit well with her. It was like seeing herself on him.

"Stop that," she tells him as she reaches out for his burnt hand.

Vince looks at her, confused. "Stop what?"

Leanne sighed and carefully rub Aloe Vera on the burnt fingertips. Vince tentatively reaches up to rub the crease that formed on her forehead. "I'm sorry," he says as he moves his fingers from her forehead to her cheeks.

"Would you tell me why you got moody?" She glances at him before turning her attention back to his burnt fingers.

"I got jealous," he says, truthfully.

She pauses, not expecting him to tell her the truth. She pushes back the blush and the urge to dance in joy. She sighs to get ahold of herself and holds his hand gently. "Why were you jealous?"

"It's nothing," he waves it off and moves to fix their dinner, but Leanne pulls him back. He sighs when he sees that she is waiting for him. "I don't want anyone to see your smile."

Leanne raises an eyebrow at him. She mentally claps herself for not squealing like an obscene teenager. "Forget it," he interrupts whatever she was supposed to say next. "I'm being selfish and obviously— "

"Good," she says to him. Vince stared at her, making sure that he heard her right. "Be jealous," she says.

"Why?"

She simply shrugs at him and turns her back to him. Every second with her is a mystery, and Vince is intrigued.

"You look different."

Leanne looks up from her computer to glance at her workmate, Kate, who is leaning on her table. She was in the middle of revising an important report when Kate suddenly bombarded her with the question. "What do you mean?" she asks, confused.

Kate waves a hand towards her. "You look different, and you are wearing a red shirt!"

"So?" She glances at the said shirt and back to Kate, not understanding at all. "What does that even mean?"

"We've been working together for five years, right?" Leanne nods at her question in agreement. She then continues, "And in those five years that we've been working together, your wardrobe palates are blue, black, and orangey-brown but never red. So, tell me. Why are you wearing red? Hmm? Anything you want to tell me?"

She raises an eyebrow at her friend's wagging one. She never knew Kate can be this nosy. She contemplates answering her questions. What should she tell her? That she woke up one day and realized that she wanted to try something new? That she wanted to verge out of her comfort zone? Kate wouldn't buy it. She opted to lie. "All my clothes are in the laundry, and this is the only shirt available."

Kate shook her, sensing her lie. "Not buying it."

She sighs and continue her work. "Good luck, then."

"Oh, come on!" Kate groans at her. "I'm too curious to sit still. Is it a guy or you are going through a rebel phase? Oh my gosh. Don't tell me you're dying!"

"A rebel phase?" she says, appalled. "Who wears red on a rebel phase?"

"You." Kate shrug. "So … is it a guy?"

Leanne momentarily pauses, not knowing what to say. Kate is right. It is because of Vince. She recalled back three days ago when Vince had a sleepover at her place. After making sure that his burnt fingers were treated, she called for takeout since their dinner for that night was on the floor. Nothing happened much afterward. They both ate their dinner with a light atmosphere in contrast to what happened ten minutes ago. Vince insisted that he should sleep on the couch in the living room, and when she woke up the following day, he was already out of the door.

The disappointment that she felt upon learning that he left was replaced with happiness when she saw her usual Starbucks drink on the kitchen table with a note.

Have class at 10 and didn't want to wake you up.

Ps. I hope I ordered the right drink. Your friends told me this was always the drink you order at Starbucks

PSS. This drink reminds me of your hair btw. – Vince

She scoffs, unable to hide her grin and the warm feeling that is slowly thawing her cold heart. She studies his note and notices that he wrote in a neat Caps lock. She grabbed bread and her drink before heading to the living room. She reached for her phone and noticed that it was close to lunch already. Is his class done? Instead of calling him, she sent him a message instead.

Leanne: Thank you.

They have been messaging and calling each other since then. She slowly gets to know Vince as the days passed by. Leanne noticed that Vince put emoticons in every message he sends. His exclamation point should always be excessive, especially if he's trying to make a point. He doesn't just type 'HAHAHA!' if he's guffawing, and most importantly, if he realizes that she's getting tired from all typing, he will call her. It always wonders her how he knows that she doesn't want to type anymore.

This should annoy her, especially the emoticons, but she finds it cute and funny at the same time. It was like a fresh breeze of air in her winter night or light after days of darkness. It was something she never thought that she needed.

Since their schedules conflict with one another, they can't meet. Speaking of schedules.

"Kate," she calls her when the latter decided to return to her desk and stop questioning her when she realized that Leanne isn't going to say anything. "I'll clock out at five."

Kate perks up and slides her swivel chair towards her table. "You. You'll clock out at five?"

She nods. She's planning to surprise Vince at the University. Kate gape at her openly. She wanted to laugh at her friend's expression. Her amusement is short-lived when Kate just stares at her. She waves a hand at her face, and the latter flinch.

"You okay?" she asks, concerned.

"You..." Leanne jumps from her chair when Kate suddenly stands up and goes to their analysis area. "Everyone! Lee is going to clock out at five!"

Leanne covers her mouth to hide her smile when the others started to shout their surprise at the news.

"What?"

"Disapprove!"

"She's a workaholic!"

"She needs to be admitted in a mental institution ASAP."

To add to their chaotic banter, she decided to tease them more. "I'm going to meet a guy!" She yells at them and lets out a quiet laugh at the hoots and exclamations that followed.

"The world is ending!"

"Dan, slap me! Oh, shit! It hurts, fucker!"

"You asked me to slap you!"

"She really needs to be admitted."

Leanne shakes her head at their comments and continues her work. She has to finish all her backlogs to clock out early. She can feel her excitement bubbles as the clock slowly heads to five. After sending her last mail for the day, she glances at the clock to see that she only has ten minutes left before she can leave.

"Ooh." Kate taunts her when she sees Leanne sorting up the papers at her table. "Excited to see your lover boy?"

She scoffs at her and continues to fix her things. "Loverboy? Really? Very original."

"What? The boys call him that."

Leanne raises an eyebrow at her statement. "Is the news of me meeting a guy really that shocking to everyone?"

Kate glances at the empty analysis area, making sure that they are alone before turning to her. "Lee, not to be offensive or anything, but I've known you for three years, and not once did we see you date anyone. Everybody thinks you are a lesbian! You might not notice it, but these past few days, you don't brood a lot."

"I don't brood."

"You do," her co-worker sigh and shrugs. "I'm actually relieved that you're finally dating. We are actually."

Leanne shakes her head at her friend's statement. She never knew that her friend was that concerned about her wellbeing. Before she leaves her friend, she sends her a soft smile. "Thank you."

Kate stands rooted to her spot when Leanne sent her that smile. When she heard the slam of the door, only then did she escape the trance that Leanne's smile sent her to. She hurriedly catches up to her and yells at her friend's back. "Lee! What was that?"

Instead of answering her, Leanne lifts her hand for a wave before turning a corner to clock out. Kate was left gaping at her back. She can't help but feel worried at that smile. Was that even a smile? Why is she smiling? Is that woman dying?

Kate was left more confused than ever.

"Thank you."

Leanne paid for the cab that dropped her off at Vince's university. It seems like searching for Vince's class isn't that hard after all. A few questions here and there from some students. They willingly point her towards his room.

As she rounds up a corner that a student pointed for her, she halts. Vince is animatedly talking to a woman. She doesn't want to conclude anything, but overthinking has been her second nature. In fact, according to Dr. Lynn, overthinking is one of the defense mechanisms she builds around herself. And the sight of Vince and that woman laughing and hugging …?

She can feel her chest tighten with emotions that aren't familiar to her at all. This is why she doesn't—never—*ever* venture out of her comfort zone. When she thought everything was going well, something or *someone* has to slap it back at her face. Wearing red, clocking out early, and surprising someone was not her. That was the version she made for herself if she stepped out of her zone. A fraud. A fake identity she assembles for somebody's pleasure.

She met a guy who pushed her to be adventurous. Someone who slowly cripples the barriers she built around herself to avoid pain, resentment, disappointment, and rejection. She hates unorganized schedules, she hates conflicts, she hates trying new things, she hates things that aren't within her control. But Vince is different. So different from her. In science, opposites attract one other. It doesn't work for the two of them. It is some random bullshit people made up to ease their minds about something that is out of their reach. They can never get along, and Leanne realized that as she became too comfortable and dependent on Vince that whatever emotion she's feeling right now is slowly ripping her from the inside.

She pats her chest to calm herself down when she felt her anxiety slowly build-up, making her nauseous. She can feel invisible walls closing on her and a grip on her throat, making her claustrophobic. She needs to leave since Vince hasn't noticed her yet, but her shoes made a squeaking sound that made Vince glance in her direction.

Vince looks up from talking to his fellow professor when he hears a sound. He glances to see a hair with a red tip walking away from him. He only knew one person with that same shade of red. He excuses himself and runs after the woman who is also running away from him.

"Leanne!"

Instead of slowing down, she hastens her pace while Vince also speeds up to catch her. Luck is not on her side when she didn't see any means of transportation to leave the university. She glances for a cab, but there isn't one in sight.

"Motherfucker," she pants under her breath when she hears footsteps slowly closing in on her.

Dr. Lynn always tells her to face her problems head-on, but this is Vince. Someone, she doesn't know how to face. Someone unpredictable. So, instead of facing him, she keeps her back to him while she calls for an Uber. But before she can dial the number, her phone is snatched from her.

"Hey!" She turns ready to slap the person but stops when she sees Vince holding her phone up in one hand as a shield and the other hand raised as if saying wait as he pants.

"Gods." He takes a deep breath to control his breathing. "You run fast, Sweetheart."

There is it again. That stupid nickname is slowly melting her like ice cream on a summer day. She should hate the nickname because it was too corny and sweet, but she fucking likes it. She pushes those thoughts away and builds her breaking fortress up when Vince called her sweetheart.

"Give me back my phone," she says through clench teeth, reaching for her phone, but Vince moves the phone away from her reach.

"No." Vince moves the hand that is holding her phone over his head. He looks down at her and internally smiles when he sees her sending daggers at his hand. She barely reaches his neck, but when he wraps his arms around her, she is just the right size and height for him. Like she is made to fit his uneven frame.

"Give. Me. Back. My. Phone!" she grits through clenched teeth.

"I will hand you back your phone, unless you tell me why you are running away from me."

Leanne scoffs at him and makes a futile attempt in reaching for her phone. He's a damn post. "Who says I'm running away from you?"

He sends her an 'are-you-kidding-me' look. She hates it when he reads her like an open book. Vince wants to crave in and hand her back her phone when he sees how annoyed she is already but at the same time, he likes the emotions that he sees on her. This was the only way he can read what was in her mind.

"Fine!" Leanne concedes. "You win."

Vince mentally smiles at her statement. "So..."

"So?"

He drops his smile and looks at her with an unpretentious look. Leanne holds her breath when she sees the change in Vince's expression. It doesn't sit well with her. She is used to him always smiling at her that this expression on him scares her. This is what her co-workers feel like when she sends them the same look that Vince is giving her right now.

She moves a bit away from him and refuses to make eye contact with him. She's not ready to face him if he's like this. She wants the smiling Vince back. She clears her throat when she feels something clogs her throat, and tears start to form on the edge of her eyes.

She looks up at the clear skies when she feels that her tears threaten to fall. She refuses to cry in front of him. She closes her eyes and takes a deep breath. Vince watches her control her emotions. Just when he thought he made it past her walls, he pushed her, and he's back to square one.

And just like a snap, she built her walls. He sighs in defeat. Blank soulless brown eyes meet his sad ones. He opens his mouth to say something, but Leanne quickly snatches her phone from him and leave him, staring at her.

He just wanted to know what was on her mind.

To know why she ran.

And to know why she's building a fortress so thick that even a single ray of sunshine can't penetrate. He thought he had seen her, get to know her. He is wrong. He hasn't even made it near her walls. He was trying so hard to reach her, but it wasn't working at all.

He sighs and tries to think of something to make it up to her. He's not giving up on her.

It was fun.

They were having fun.

Everyone, except the eldest son, was there.

It was six months after her grandfather died, and this was the second time this year that her mother's family were all present.

Christmas Eve. The happiest time of the year.

She never expected that after the fun and the laughter, shit would happen.

Leanne woke up earlier than she expected, considering that they slept past two o'clock in the morning. After she did her routine, she heads downstairs to start breakfast just like she always does when her parents are working.

She paused in her tracks when she saw her father, eating cup noodles, and her uncle sitting at the dining table. She had an eerie feeling with the way the silence enveloped the table, but she pushed it far behind her mind and approached them.

"Morning, Papa," she greeted her father first before turning to acknowledge her uncle. "Morning, Uncle."

Her uncle nodded his head in greeting and kept on sipping his coffee. She heads to the kitchen to start cooking. She was preparing the rice when she heard the scrape of the chair being pushed back. She glanced back to see her brother standing by the faucet, glancing at their father.

She frowned and returned to her cooking. She must have everything done before everyone wakes up.

"Annie."

She looked up when she heard her father call out her nickname. "James is sick. Make sure he eats at least before drinking his medicine. I have training today. Your mother is still asleep."

James is the youngest, and he's been sporting a fever for a week now. Her father's request was nothing out of the ordinary. Before she can agree, her uncle interrupted.

"Why should she do that?" he spitted out. "It's your child! You can't even cook her breakfast. You should be the one cooking their breakfast!"

Leanne glanced worriedly at her other brother, who remained standing by the sink. She saw him clench the counter tightly until his knuckles turned white. In her defense, there is nothing wrong with her father's request. She was used to those certain kinds of requests within their family, that whatever her father was requesting was normal to her or her brothers.

Instead of answering his brother-in-law's back, her father opted to remain silent and turn his back since he is running late for the training. But before her father can leave the kitchen, her uncle opened his mouth to spew out bullshit.

"Hey!" her uncle yelled. "I'm talking to you. Is this how your mother brought you up? Being disrespectful?"

With how loud her uncle's voice is, those who were asleep woke up wondering what the commotion is about. What Leanne's family didn't know was that her mother's brothers has planned this all along. One of the carpenters who was doing a house renovation to their uncle's house two days ago mentioned to Leanne's mother's older brother that one of their brothers was planning something. A royal rumble of some sort. Thinking that it won't happen during Christmas, the eldest among five siblings ignored the warning.

Despite being belittled, Leanne's father ignored her uncle which made the latter madder. Her father remained calm despite the chaos that is going on inside the house. This is one of the times that she wished that her father had fought back to defend himself. Her father was a soldier before he injured his back during one of his trips abroad.

Leanne felt something lodged in her throat at the way her uncle was treating her father. She wanted to lash out or at least step up for her father, but she did none of those. She was rooted at her spot with fear and confusion about what is happening.

She saw her brother move from his spot at the sink from her peripheral view. She captured his attention and signaled him to stay put and not interfere in the heated argument that her uncle initiated. When she thought that it was over, her other uncle joined the argument.

She looked at her father who is sporting a calm expression despite the arguments that his brothers-in-law are starting. What she was feeling was the opposite of her father. She wanted to slap them and scream at them for accusing her father of baseless things.

The argument between the adults got heated as her mother, and the wives decided to make their presence known. She didn't know how long the argument lasted but the next thing she knew, she was packing her clothes and things alongside her family.

She can hear her mother making some phone calls inquiring about a hotel vacancy.

"What do you think is going to happen next?" She stopped from taping the box that contains her books and turned her attention to her brother who witnessed everything that happened in the kitchen. She felt bad that he had to see all of those. The harsh words, baseless accusations, and the way their mother's family denigrates their father. Those were the things that a fourteen-year-old shouldn't see.

She sighed. She can' afford to break down right now and complain at how unjust everything was. Her brothers depended on her, her mother needed her, she needed to be stronger for her crumbling family. "Honestly, I don't know."

"This is not fair," he argued. "Papa only did those things they mentioned because it was an emergency! Papa didn't want to drive the car without a license, but he had to because grandma needed to be rushed to the hospital!"

Leanne gulped down the clog that got stuck in her throat. She felt her chest constrict with frightful emotions. She closed her eyes and took a deep breath to calm herself. When she felt that she had schooled and bagged her emotions away, she then prioritized her brother who is on the verge of breaking down. She grabbed his travel bag and headed to his cabinet that was still unpacked.

"Sitting here won't help us either," she said as she stuffed his bag with his clothes.

She kept on packing their clothes as her brother slowly get ahold of himself. Not even an hour had passed, they had packed and left the house with only a few days' worth of clothes. They had no idea what to do next, but Leanne was sure of one thing.

Things will never be the same for her.

"Lee!"

"Leanne!"

"Leanne!"

She wakes up gasping. Her dreams are becoming more vivid than it usually does.

"You okay?"

She glances around to see her friends sitting around her bed. She let out wheezing breathe when her breathing won't calm down. Her friends right away notice the symptoms. Janine hurriedly grabs her bag and search for a brown bag. Mary holds her head up while Anne reaches out to grab her freezing hands that are slowly contracting from the lack of oxygen.

Her friends try to calm her down, but the pounding in her ears is so loud that she can't hear anything. Leanne taught them what to do in case she suddenly starts to hyperventilate, but none of it was working. Scared and distraught that their friend is getting worst. Her breathing is becoming shallow, and she's shivering uncontrollably. Janine intuitively grabs her friend's phone.

"What are you doing?" Anne asks Janine when she reach out to grab Leanne's hand.

Janine presses her friend's finger for her biometrics, and with shaky hands, she searches for Dr. Lynn's number. "Calling for help."

"Leanne—"

"Help," Janine interrupts Dr. Lynn. "Leanne … she's … she-she's … she's getting worse."

Dr. Lynn frowned when an unfamiliar voice answered. She double-checks her phone to see that it is Leanne who is calling her. "May I know who's speaking?"

"It's Janine," the person on the other line sniffs like she's been crying. "Leanne's friend."

Dr. Lynn recalls from her sessions with Leanne that Janine is one of her friends who knew about her condition. "What is—"

"She's not calming down," Leanne's friend cries, distraught. "She's shivering too much. She … she is wheezing."

"Calm down. If you panic, you won't be able to help her," Dr. Lynn calms the person on the other line. "Have you given her any medications?"

"No."

"Good. Janine, right?" Dr. Lynn waits for the affirmative answer before continuing, "call 911. I'll meet you there in a few. Do you understand?"

Janine immediately drops the call and dials 911.

"911, what's your emergency?"

Vince paces back and forth in his study, sending daggers to his phone that is resting on his table. He's hesitating to call Leanne. He is stupid enough to push her. He got impatient that he forced her to express what was on her mind. He forgot that Leanne is someone who is used to pushing people away. Someone who keeps everyone around her at arm's length.

He sighs and runs his finger through his hair in frustration. He turns to his cat that is taking a nap on his swivel chair. "Should I call her?"

Kutch blinks at him before turning his back to him. "Very useful," he grumbles and continues pacing back and forth.

He finally made up his mind. He's about to grab his phone when it rings. He takes a deep breath to calm himself, and not to appear as he waited for her call. But his excitement crashes down when he sees that it is Deo, who's calling him.

He grumpily answers the call. "Hello," he didn't bother hiding his disappointment.

"Were you expecting someone else?" His friend laughs on the other line.

"I was," he grumbles. "What do you want?"

Deo sighed, and Vince knew what that sigh meant. "The wedding will push through."

"And?" He rubs his forehead.

"*And* I don't want to get married to a stranger!"

He sighs and leans on his study table. "Deo, she wouldn't have been a stranger if only you didn't stand her up several times!"

"But I don't want to get to know her."

His irritation fires up to the roof at his friend's words. He and Deo had this argument, over and over again that it's starting to irritate him. "What is your point, Deo?" He snaps.

As if sensing his irritation, Deo sighed. "I'm sorry. This whole wedding thing is stressing me out. Sorry for taking it out on you."

Vince rubs his nape. "Sorry for snapping."

"Well…"

"What is it?" When his friend remains silent. "Spit it out, Deo, or I'm dropping the call."

"I need you company."

Vince's forehead scrunches in confusion. "For what?"

"I'm going to stalk her, and I need your opinion about her."

His eyebrows raise when he hears his friend's request. This is a first. Deo's family must have threatened him for him to act differently towards his potential bride. To quench his curiosity, he agreed to his friend's shenanigan.

Thirty minutes later, Vince found himself inside Deo's car, heading towards a hospital. He glances at the hospital before turning towards his friend, who is looking for a parking spot near the doors. "Can you please explain to me why we are in a hospital?"

Deo places the car in park before turning to his confused friend. "My great lovely mother told me that she's a nurse in this hospital."

"Did it ever occur to you that she might be busy right now?"

His friend shrugs. "We aren't going to talk to her anyway. We'll just take a peek then leave."

"I don't know who I should pity more. You, your mom, or your fiancée."

Instead of answering him, his friend opens the door and gestures for him to do the same. Vince tentatively unfastens his seatbelt and follows his friend, who is walking ahead of him already. He's really starting to question his decision right now. He quietly follows his friend, who seems to know where to find his fiancée.

After a few rounds and turns, they finally reach Deo's fiancée's department. They both head to the nurse's station, and he let Deo do all the talking.

"Excuse me?" he hears Deo call the nurse's attention. "Is Nurse Ava Brila around?"

"Yes, she's in Room 356."

"Thank you."

He turns to his friend with a knowing smirk. "So ... you remembered her name?"

Deo shrugs like it's nothing important. "Her name's easy to remember."

He raises an eyebrow at him, taunting him. "You never bother to remember your previous fiancées' names. What changed?"

"Nothing," Deo frowns at his friend's waggling eyebrows. "We are simply stalking her."

"Stalking?" He grins wider at his friend's way of dodging his questions. "Does stalking involves remembering her name and her work?"

If looks could kill, Vince will be six feet under with the way Deo is glaring at him. He laughs at his friend's unease and decides to leave it for later. They both left the nurse's station and headed to the room where Deo's fiancée is. When they finally find the corridor where the room is, Vince stops which made Deo turn to him, confused as to why he suddenly stops.

"You, okay?" Deo asks his friend.

Vince acts like he doesn't hear his friend, he did, but he just doesn't know how to answer that question when he sees Leanne's friends in front of the room that Deo's fiancée is assigned to. His heart is beating arduously in his chest when he realizes that Leanne isn't with them.

He dashes in their direction, leaving his friend bewildered at his reaction. He is close enough to hear their conversation and what he heard made him stagger.

"We have to sedate her if she won't calm down. She's still asleep, and we've contacted her psychiatrist. All we have to do is wait for her to wake up."

What happened?

"Vince?"

The trance that he is in shatters when his friend calls his name, making Leanne's friends look in their direction. He sees the shock in their faces, and they glance at one another in a silent message wondering if they should tell him or not.

Deo grabs his friend's hand before he can take one step. "Bro, what's going on?" He asks, bothered by the way Vince suddenly freezes when he sees the three people outside of the room his fiancée is assigned to.

"Vince?" One of them voices out.

"You knew this people?" Deo whispers to him, but he ignores him and walks closer to Leanne's friends.

"Hey," he says, tentatively. "Where's Leanne?"

They glance at one another before the tallest one gestures for him to follow her. She leads towards the door that he and Deo were looking for. She pauses her hand like she's going to knock and turns to him. She gauges him, and the way she's assessing him is enough to refreeze the polar caps that had melted due to global warming.

She opens the door, and the sight that met him grips his chest so tight that it became suffocating. While he was feeling disappointed for not receiving a call from her, Leanne is in the hospital fighting a silent battle that she's currently losing.

He urges himself to move, but Leanne's friend stops him. "I don't know if meeting you is the best thing that happened to Lee or the worst thing. She changed a lot when she met you." She turns her attention to Vince, who remains staring at Leanne's immobile body. "Humor me,

Vince. Why should I let you see my friend when you can be the cause of her downfall?"

He doesn't have an answer to her question. He can't remove his gaze at her unmoving body as Deo's fiancée writes her chart. She looks different compared to when he last saw her. She's much paler and frailer. Her fiery red tips seem to lose their luster. Vince can't help but feel that it was all his fault.

He licks his dry lips and answers the person beside him without taking his eye off Leanne's sleeping form. "To tell you the truth … I don't know how to answer that question."

Anne frowns at him. She wants to know his intentions with her friend. She's concerned about her friend's well-being, and ever since she met Vince her condition worsens.

"You better have an answer to that question," she says before turning her back to him. "Because if you are only with Lee out of pity or the thrill of it or worst, for a research project, I suggest you leave her right now. My friend has been through so much growing up, she doesn't need any of your bullshit lame excuses of being with her."

Pity?

Thrill?

Research project?

Those never crossed his mind. He wants to be with Leanne because of who she is. He wants to be there during her highs and lows. He wants to see her smile and laugh at his lame attempt at making jokes. He wants to be the shoulder she leans on when she is sad and to hug her when she's having bad days.

He loves her enough to embrace her darkness and give her warm during the coldest nights.

He loves her.

Vince staggers back with the realization. It was like a thorn was plucked out from him at the realization. It's a calming warmth that embraces him and waiting to be shared. There is one person that he is willing to share this feeling with.

It is then, he realizes that the nurse had also left the room, leaving him and Leanne alone. Cautiously, he takes a step towards Leanne. He doesn't know what to feel when he held her cold hands. It was too much for him to handle in one day.

Everything is in shambles.

The smell of antiseptic greats Leanne when she slowly arouses. She lets out a rough cough when she suddenly takes a deep breath.

"Leanne." She hears Vince's voice. She must be dreaming. When her cough finally subsides, she opens her eyes and was immediately greeted by white walls. White walls? Her room isn't this shade of white. She roams her eyes around the surroundings, and she sees an IV drip hanging on top of her left shoulder. There is a white hospital band on her left wrist with her details. She is wearing a hospital gown that smells strongly of disinfectants.

"Sweetheart."

She sees Vince sitting beside her with his hand on the edge of her bed. Why is he here? Why is she in the hospital? What happened?

"Sweetheart?" Vince calls out to her when he sees that she's close to having a panic attack.

Skeptically, he reaches out to hold her cold hand. "Calm down."

She turns to him and lets herself be drowned by his warm chocolate eyes. She can feel her breathing slowly turn back to normal, and she continues to stare at him. His eyes hold promises and futures that made her want to experience it with him but at the same frightens her.

He holds a cup filled with water towards her. "Drink this first."

She whispers a soft, hoarse thank you and gulps the water in one go. She lets out a sigh of relief when the water hits her parched throat. She hands the cup back to Vince. "One more."

"Please."

Vince smiles at the way she tilts her head in confusion. He holds up the cup, and she immediately realizes what he was implying. She sends him a smile and says, "Please?"

He momentarily forgot what he was supposed to do when she flashed him a smile. He's calling it the Leanne effect. A phenomenon where he loses his shit when she smiles and laughs. He almost said the L-word to her. It's not the time yet.

"Vince? Vince?" She waves a hand in front of him when he became immobile. She chuckles at his awestruck emotion. Does her smile really affect him that much? She should smile more often if it has this effect on Vince.

She then remembers what happened in the university when she visited Vince. She feels an invisible hand grips her chest at the sudden onslaught of negative emotions. She was jealous. Leanne is taken back with that realization. She was jealous of the woman. She wasn't jealous of the woman's beauty; she was jealous at the way she glows, the way she smiles like she doesn't have a weight on her shoulders. She smiles so carefreely, like someone who wasn't traumatized by her past. Someone worth it of him.

Vince sees the smile from her face slowly fade. He silently watches her. He sees how she looks anywhere but him. Her fingers play with the sheets to keep them busy, and he sees how her breathing became hollow. He then heard her sniff.

He places the cup on the table beside her bed before holding one of her restless hands. It is so cold. "Sweetheart?"

"Stop," she says in a broken voice. Doesn't deserve that nickname. "Stop calling me that."

She needs to get answers from him, but his calling her makes her weak and soft for him. She keeps her face away from him. She doesn't want him to see her crying so pettily over something as simple as jealousy. She doesn't have the right to be jealous. She doesn't have any hold over Vince, nor they are dating.

The thought of Vince dating someone else made her cry more. Just the idea of him leaving her or ignoring her made her chest tighten with sadness that she could not explain. She hates it. She hates feeling this way.

Vince wraps his hands on hers to spread a little bit of warmth to her cold ones. "Leanne," he begs in the softest voice he can muster. "Talk to me, please."

Please.

Vince said please. She hates it. Vince shouldn't beg certainly not for her attention.

Despite tears running down her face, she turns to face Vince, who greeted her with a smile. She doesn't deserve his smiles. She doesn't deserve his time. His patience, most definitely, she doesn't deserve him.

But, for once in her life, she wants to be selfish. She wants to be better. She's tired of being sick all the time. She's tired of the nightmares, and she's tired of being stuck in the past.

She wants to see the world without the lingering feeling of sadness. She wants to be genuinely happy without any ounce of regret afterward. In order to do that, she has to face her demons. She has to be brave and confident. The trip to the hospital is her wake-up call.

Vince reaches out to wipe her tears away. It pains him to see her crying but what she says next made his worry disappear. "Don't beg," she says, rubbing her thumb on the back of his hand. "Don't beg."

"I have to get your attention somehow," he says, rubbing the path where her tears used to be. "You won't look at me."

She closes her eyes and rubs her cheek against his thumb. She likes the warmth that envelopes her with his simple action. "I don't want you to see me cry."

"Silly girl," he chuckles under his breath. "How can I be the shoulder you get to lean on when you won't even let me see you cry? It's okay to pretend in front of other people, but, Leanne, I want to see you. All of you. So, don't hide from me. Okay?"

"But it's going to be ugly."

"Who told you that I want it to be pretty?" He smiles at her and holds her two hands with his. "I don't care if it's going to be ugly or broken. I want to be with you. I want to see all your darkness and pain. I want to be your shoulder when you feel like you can't carry the world. I want to be the only medicine you need when you have your moments. But you have to give me a chance, Sweetheart. Just try?"

She moves to sit up, and Vince assists her. Her grip in his hand tightens when he tried to move. After hearing his confession, Leanne doesn't want to let him go. Physically and emotionally. But before she answers his confession, she too has a confession to make.

"I lied," she whispers, embarrass at her action.

Confused, Vince asks. "About what?"

She glances at him before looking away. She can't look at him while the guilt is gnawing inside of her. She doesn't want to see the disappointed look on Vince's face when she tells him her lie. "Remember when I asked you to sleepover?" When he nods, she continues. "I wasn't feeling well that day because of a nightmare. I... I couldn't calm down no matter what grounding technique I did. So, I took a pill."

Vince didn't know how to feel about her confession. He remains calm. "Have you taken any pill afterward?"

She shakes her head no. "That was the only time I drank a pill after meeting you."

"How often do you usually take your pill?"

"Once a month?" She shrugs. "Sometimes twice depending on how severe my moments are."

He rubs his fingers along her hand. "Will you…" He pauses and sighs. "When you're ready, can you tell me what triggers those moments?"

Leanne intertwines their fingers together. She smiles when she notices how her small and slim fingers fit his larger ones. No pun intended. She nods. "I will." She lifts their hands together and presses a kiss on the back of his hand. And, with firmness, she says. "I will."

Vince's smile hasn't left his face ever since she woke up. Without thinking of any consequence, his body moves on its own accord. He leans in and presses his lips on hers. Leanne gasped in surprise, and Vince grab it as an opportunity to deepen the kiss.

He's kissing her.

It takes a while before everything sinks into Leanne. She doesn't have any experience in the kiss department, but she follows Vince's lead. Her lips are soft and taste like chocolates and solitude, no butterflies or sparks were flying. There was only peace and silence. Two things that she struggles to achieve, but with Vince, only he can make all her demons quiet down.

All the thoughts, the fears, and expectations, Leanne pours it into the kiss. Her hand that was holding Vince's hand is on his nape, pulling him much closer to her. There isn't any space between, but it wasn't enough.

The need to breathe urges Vince to let go of Leanne's lips. The latter whines in protest and connects their lips again. She doesn't want to let go of him. But a knock on the door forces her to let go of Vince's addicting lips.

Leanne smiles when she sees Vince's bruised lips. She did that. She moves to capture Vince's lips again but is interrupted by a knock on the door again. When none of them bothered to move, the knocking became persistent, and Vince sighed in annoyance.

"Whoever is on the other side of that door better have a good reason for interrupting us," Leanne murmur, slightly distancing herself from Vince.

"Sweetheart," he says in a reprimanding tone.

She sighs and sulks as Vince heads to open the door. And lo behold her friends standing by the door frame with sly smirks on their faces.

Mary speaks up, "What did we miss?"

Tomato is a Berry. Berry is a Fruit. Tomato is a Fruit.

She was confined at the hospital for three days. Three long days. Dr. Lynn made her stay for an extra day to make sure that she cleared all of her "psychiatric exams" before signing her discharge papers. She wouldn't have agreed to that extra day because she was itching to go home already. The thought of her unfinished work and school assignments made her edgy, but Dr. Lynn asked Vince to convince her to stay. Dr. Lynn finally figured out her kryptonite.

Her psychiatrist would use Vince to make her cooperative of their sessions, and Vince, his good poor soul, was glad to be helpful in Leanne's recovery. Dr. Lynn made her promise that if she ever had those nightmares again, she would call her.

"You know I can walk, right?" Leanne says to Vince as he pushes the wheelchair towards the hospital exit. "I don't need a wheelchair."

"I know, Sweetheart," Vince sigh at her complain. "Protocol."

Leanne pouts but doesn't barter back. She knew that Vince is starting to be annoyed at her complaints ever since her discharge papers were signed. She decided to let him push her wheelchair in silence. She hates an annoyed Vince. She hates it when Vince isn't smiling, and the latter knew it. Just like Dr. Lynn, he uses her weakness against her.

Damn, that man can read her like a book all the time.

"What do you want for dinner?" Vince asks her when they reach his car in the parking lot.

She wears her seatbelt before facing him. Whatever she was going to say was held back as she watches him reverse his car out of the parking lot. She blatantly checks him out. He's wearing a blue sweatshirt and khaki pants. His hair is slightly disheveled with the number of times he runs his hand through his hair in frustration. He's wearing reading glasses, and it does wonders to her.

She can see nurses and visitors brazenly ogle at him when they passed by the hospital corridors, but he didn't even throw them a glance.

However, she pettily glared at them as if saying, 'That is my man. Back off, bitches.'

Vince glance at her when she doesn't answer him for quite some time and see her staring at him. When she realizes that he catches her staring at him, a bright shade of red covers her whole face. Cute, Vince thought as she quickly hides her face away from him by staring at the window.

"You know," he can't help but tease her. "You can stare at me all you want, Sweetheart. I'm all yours."

At his admonition, her face heats up more. "I'm not staring at you."

"Still not stopping you," she can hear the laughter at his tone.

"Vince," she warns and glares at him. "Shut up."

He zips his mouth at her warning and laughs silently when she sulks beside him. Who knew she could be sensitive to jokes? He noticed that after their kiss, she became a bit vocal with her thoughts. There are still times that she hides, especially if she's mad or in a crowd of strangers.

But those baby steps are enough for him to know that she's trying.

"Sweetheart?" he calls her. "What do you want to eat?"

"Can we order take out?" She's craving some fried chicken from McDonald's. She kind of missed the food outside of the hospital. These past few days, all she ever ate were tasteless foods. Isn't table salt a thing in the hospital kitchen?

He winces. "You just got out of the hospital, and you want to eat junk food?"

She rolls her eyes at him. "I'm craving for a burger."

"That's not healthy."

"How is that not healthy?" She turns to him and holds up a finger every time she makes a point. "One, it has carbohydrates. Two, it has meat for protein, and lastly, it has vegetables because lettuce, tomato, and onion are a vegetable."

"In case you forgot, Sweetheart." He smiles at her before stopping at a red light. "Tomato is a fruit."

"Eh?"

He nods, stepping on the gas. "Ask Google."

Not trusting him with the new information, Leanne takes out her phone and types:

Is tomato a fruit?

She mentally curses when she sees the article saying that the tomato is basically a berry. She pretends to glare at him, but deep inside, she is cheering when she heard him chuckle.

She sounds like a lovesick girlfriend.

Wait...

She rummages inside herself to see if the idea of falling in love or being in a relationship with Vince still scares her. When her anxiety levels remain normal, and she can't find any fear at the thought of being attached to someone, she smiles at Vince.

If they were still on the road, they would have been in an accident since Vince was startled when Leanne suddenly smiled at him. This isn't the first time that Leanne smiled at him, but this is the first time that Leanne beamed at him. Her smile stretches on her face that it reached her ears.

Unable to help himself, he removes his seatbelt and leans in to capture her smile. Leanne didn't hesitate to wrap her hands at his neck to pull him closer.

Vince's kisses send a euphoric feeling to her dull world. A breeze of warm air to her cold days. Screw those butterflies and fireworks. This is what she needs, warmth, comfort, and peace.

This is what home feels like. Her home smells like mint and lemon.

I love you.

She pulls away from Vince's tempting lips when those words pop into her mind. She loves him. With those thoughts in her mind, she moves away from the bubble that Vince made in her mind.

What if he doesn't feel the same way?

What is she going to do if Vince doesn't feel the same way? She's going to be ruined. She's in too deep in this emotion that it's harder to swim away from it.

Vince grabs her hand when she's starting to pick on the skin on her fingers. One step forward. Two steps back. Vince reprimanded himself when a sudden feeling of impatience grew inside of him.

"Sweetheart?" he calls her attention.

"I'm sorry," she blurts out.

Vince tightens his hold on her hand. "Why?" he says in confusion.

"For pulling away," she says, agitated. "I know I said I'm going to try to be better, but the voice is saying about doubting my feelings, and they are telling me that I l—"

She stops rambling, and her eyes widen when she realizes that she almost blurted out that she loves him. No…

"That you what, Sweetheart?"

Oh, shit. She has to think quick or else he will know that she's planning to lie. "That I want to be your girlfriend."

Shit.

Leanne mentally slaps herself when she recalled what she blurted out at Vince's car.

"That I want to be your girlfriend."

Was that the best cover-up that she could think of? To make it even worst, Vince remained taciturn, and haven't spoken a word to her.

When they arrived at her apartment, he immediately heads to the kitchen like he can't wait to be away from her. Stupid, Leanne.

Instead of following him to the kitchen, she heads to her room to take a quick shower to remove the scent of disinfection that's clinging to her skin. When she had finally changed into her comfy pajamas, she decided to head to the kitchen to see what Vince is doing.

She sees him standing with his back to her. She is about to call his attention when he speaks up.

"I don't know, man," he sounds exasperated. "She's different."

They were talking about her. Vince pauses, listening to whoever is on the other side of the phone while running his hands through his hair. Leanne finds it sexy and troubling at the same time because he only touches his hair when he's annoyed or frustrated.

She moves to make herself known, but what he said next broke her. I . . .felt impatient a while ago while she almost had a breakdown. I know. Why do you think I'm trying to understand her? She refuses to let me in, man, no matter how patient I am with her. Yeah, she is. You, too. Night."

Leanne can hear her heart-shattering in her ears. Just when she finally accepts what she feels for him . . .this is why she built her walls. To avoid feeling like the whole world is against her.

She was stupid in thinking that maybe she could crumble the walls that she tried so hard to build bit by bit over a man who would never accept her feelings. People do stupid things for the people they love.

She held a hand to her chest when she felt it constrict with unshed tears. She refuses to show him that she is the effect of what he said. She refuses to let him see her walls slowly crumble with the unbearable weight that it has been holding.

She was supposed to get better. What did she do to deserve this? Doesn't she deserve to be happy for once?

As if sensing her internal battle, Vince turns toward her position. Upon seeing her detached expression, he knew she heard him and misunderstood what he said to Deo.

The reason he called Deo was to ask for advice on how to woo Leanne. But clearly, Leanne only heard the last part of their conversation where he has to explain to Deo why he has to be patient in handling Leanne.

She's the strongest person that he knew but the most fragile woman he ever met. She is one of a kind and different. Would he wish he fell for someone uncomplicated and less emotional luggage?

NO.

But first, he has to woo her and explain his side. Vince moves to explain when a phone ring out of nowhere. Leanne thanked all the holy who are currently at her side when she heard her phone ring. And whoever is ever on the other side of the phone deserves a treat for saving her from a consequential conversation with Vince.

She knows that they have to talk about what she heard but as of the moment, running and avoiding is the only thing in her mind.

Vince sighed in annoyance when Leanne left to answer the phone. Just when everything is going great, he has to mess it all up. While waiting for her to return back to the kitchen, he decided to arrange their meal. They will have a conversation before he leaves her apartment. Whether she wants it or not, she has to let him explain.

What Does it Mean if Something is Consequential?

Leanne is a bit disappointed when she left Vince in the kitchen to answer her boss's call. She knows that despite being patient with her, Vince will grow tired of waiting for her.

He is the most patient and the calmest person she met, but when will it last? Before the ring ends, she answers the call. "Boss?"

"Oh, Lee," her boss says, shock that she answered the call. "How are you?"

"I'm doing okay." She's hardly okay. She's confused and vexed at how she handled the situation back in the kitchen.

"Anne told me that you just got out of the hospital?"

"Yeah."

"Do you feel like talking?"

Cold feelings crawl at her spine at her boss's question. It was as if he knew about her condition. She made Anne swear to her not to tell anyone the reason why she was rushed to the hospital. But it seems like she slipped and told her boss.

She acted like she had no idea what her boss was implying. "I'm doing okay, Boss. The doctor told me to take it easy."

"Lee…"

She cut him off before he can say anything. "I'll be back to work in a week."

And quickly end the call. She hears it chime with a message, but she doesn't bother to read the message. She drops her head on her lap and groans out loud.

This is so messed up.

She takes a deep breath and stows away any emotions that she has on her face before heading to the kitchen. She has to be strong in dealing with Vince right now because one-touch or smile from him will melt her.

She sees him staring at the plate vacantly. The table is set for two, and Vince is standing at the side of the table facing her while his hands are gripping the edges of the table.

The emotions that she stored somewhere a while ago resurface at the troubled look on his face. He isn't smiling, nor did he hold a calm expression. In place is a blank canvass that she claims is hers.

She moves stealthily towards him. She's not sure if he heard her or not, but he didn't move an inch. Only when she's standing beside him did he move to face her.

His face is desolate of any emotions. He never looked at her this way, even when she was showing him the same expression to him every time.

So, this is what it feels like to be the receiving end of that look. It was scary and unforeseeable.

All she wanted was to erase that look on Vince. She wants her calm and level-headed Vince. This is the side of him that she hasn't seen yet, and it leaves an unsettling feeling in her gut.

"Babe...?" She tentatively wraps her arms around his waist and buries her face at the side of his arm. He smells lemony, and the lid of all her pent-up emotions opens. She feels him stiffen, but she ignores it and burrows her face into his body. She doesn't realize that she's bawling her eyes out, and Vince was consoling her like he always does. It made Leanne cry more.

All she ever did was say, cry and pity herself while he was always calming her down and patiently waiting for her. Nobody would do that, nobody but Vince.

"I'm sorry," she cries. "I'm sorry if I make you wait for me to get better. I'm sorry if I don't make you feel important. I'm sorry if I don't show my feelings to you. I know you are getting tired of me. But I'm really trying. I—"

Whatever she is supposed to say next disappeared when Vince smashes his lips to her. Whatever was clouding her mind a while ago disappear when Vince's lips touched hers.

His lips are soft and warm, and she doesn't hesitate to press herself closer to him. Vince deepens the kiss, and she let him. Ever since their first kiss, she started to get addicted to Vince's kisses. Like it was always never enough.

I love you.

I love you.

She's the first one to let go of his lips. She's panting while staring at his red, soft, plump lips. She felt a sense of achievement knowing that she did that.

When that sinks in, her face heats up in embarrassment, and she hides her flaming face from Vince, who is confused why she's pressing herself to him more, and then he remembers what she called him.

Babe...

He turns to Leanne, who is still burrowing her face in his chest. Cute. He smiles at her gesture. As much as he likes having her close to him, he has to confirm something first.

"Sweetheart?" He cups her face and lilts it up so that he can look at her while he asks his question, but Leanne won't meet his eyes. So, he hardens his tone, which works, especially when she's being hardheaded. "Sweetheart."

He can feel her stiffen at the way he calls her. She slowly meets his eyes, and he has to put much effort into keeping the expression on his face. Otherwise, he's going to melt at the warry expression on her face.

He notices that her eyes aren't as cold and blank as the first time he saw her. It is still a little hollow, but he can see a certain emotion to it that reflects his.

He dares hope so.

"What did you call me?" he asks, slowly now that he got her attention.

"What?" Her eyebrows raise at his question. Her mind is still foggy with their kiss that she doesn't acknowledge his question.

"Before you babble and apologize?"

She squirms at his scrutiny. She racks up her brain as to what he was talking about. Vince watches her forehead scrunch in concertation. Her eyes widen when she finally realized what he was talking about.

Babe.

She called him babe, an endearment. The word just went out of her mouth, and she is surprised at how familiar the word is to her. Like she's been calling Vince's babe for years and not some random outburst.

She covers her mouth at the thought. She looks at Vince, perplexed. "I'm sorry. I shouldn't have— "

"Stop," Vince interrupts her before she can start babbling some nonsense. "Stop saying sorry. What are you sorry for anyway? I should be the one to say that I'm sorry."

She looks at him, stupefied by his words. "Why should you be sorry?"

"Uh … you know … the call?"

She then figures out that she's supposed to be mad at him, and yet, here she is, in his arms, forgetting that she's supposed to be furious with him.

Vince wince at the scowl that appears on her face. He quickly explains his side. "I called Deo, my friend, a while ago. I . . . ahm…" He scratches his nape, and a bright shade of red covers his whole neck to his ears. "I… asked him for some advice."

Leanne keeps her cool even though she wants to tease his read face. She wants to squish his cheeks at how cute he is right now, but she held her stare and tone. "Didn't you say that you are tired?"

He sighs and moves away from her and sits on the chair closest to him. The action made Leanne ache. She remains standing but the cool that she was maintaining disappeared when he creates a distance between the two of them.

Vince saw the shift in her emotions. He sighs and grabs her hands instead. "Sweetheart," he pauses, thinking of the right words to say what's on his mind right now.

"Spit it out, Vince," she says impatiently.

He recoils at the way she says his name. He decided to be in candor with her. "These past few days, I've been feeling a bit of impatience or more of a disappointment at myself. Not at you. Definitely not at you, sweetheart. I've been trying to make a place in your heart for months, but I get the feeling that I'm even halfway in. Like I'm still standing behind your walls, waiting for you to open a portion to let me in.

"I know I should consider your situation," he continues as she gapes at his honesty. "But what about me? I don't know how long I'll have to wait. I'm scared, Leanne. I'm scared that one day I'll wake, and you decided that you don't want to be with me. That you won't give me a chance. I'm scared that the time will come that I'll get tired and stop understanding you. That I'll stop."

"I don't want to stop being the shoulder you'll lean on. I want to be with you and see how this relationship will go. To be honest, this is the first time that I ever felt this way. This is the first time that I actually doubt myself in terms of dating. So, I called Deo and ask for his opinion."

Leanne held her breath at what he was going to say next. She jolts when Vince's fingers brush her cheeks. Only then does she notice that tears are flowing down her cheeks.

"What did..." She clears her throat when her voice came out hoarse. "What did Deo say?"

"He asks me a question. He said, 'Is she worth it?' And I said, 'Yeah, she is.'" He smiles at her. "That was the part where you create your misconception."

She sniffs and wipes her tears away. Damn, this person. All this time, this is what is going on inside his mind. This made Leanne realize that she's taking it all for granted. It never crossed her mind that Vince would stop understanding her. She only thought that he'll get tired, but he'll never stop understanding her.

And that thought made her ache. She wraps her arms around Vince and cries, that's all she ever did. Cry and say sorry. But what if the time comes that her sorry won't be enough to convince Vince to stay.

The thought made her cry more. Ever since meeting Vince, her tear ducts are working nonstop. She hardly cries. She didn't even shed a tear when her grandpa died or when her cat died, but with Vince . . .she became a crybaby.

Vince pulls her to sit on his lap, and he rubs his palm at her back to calm her down when her cries became uncontrollable. He's worried that she'll start hyperventilating if she won't calm down.

"Sweetheart, calm down," he coos. "You'll hyperventilate if you won't calm down."

She buries her face to his neck and inhale his lemony scent that made her calm down slowly.

"You okay?" he asks, and she nods in answer.

When she finally stops crying, she turns her face to look at him. Her cheeks are wet with tears, and her eyes are swollen and red from crying. And at that moment, all Vince could think was she's the most beautiful woman he met.

"Thank you," she whispers. "For telling me."

He pulls her closer to him that she can hear his heartbeat racing. "Always, Sweetheart. Always."

"What the hell is that supposed to mean?" Leanne asks herself while she's catching up with all the schoolwork that she missed when she was admitted to the hospital.

She's only been gone from their online class for a week, but she's already having a hard time catching up with the assignments and projects that the professors assigned to them. She thought that either one of her three friends would have had made her assignments, but she was wrong. Those bitches didn't even help her.

She sighs and rubs her forehead when she still couldn't get the correct answer to the problem that she's currently solving. To whoever created the subject Statistics, screw you. If only she didn't need this subject to pass her master's degree, she wouldn't have made this kind of effort.

She sees her phone lit up in her peripheral view, and she glances at it to see that Vince sent her a message. Ignoring her works, she prioritized his message.

After the talk in her kitchen, she swore to herself that she'll be more open to Vince. She doesn't want him to give up on her, and for that to happen, she needs to let her walls down for him.

Vince: you busy?

Leanne: still doing schoolwork

Vince: oh… still?

Leanne: been at it for hours

She waits for his reply, but nothing came. She frowns when after five minutes, he still hasn't replied to her. Is he busy? She decides to shrug it off and continue her work. The fewer distractions she has, the quicker her work will be done.

She is immersed in answering her synthesis problems that she jumps in surprise when somebody knocks on the door.

She let out a shriek when a long unnecessary pen mark lined her almost-finished synthesis problem. "Oh no. Oh no. Oh no!" she chants when she realizes that the pen line covers half of her paper.

She has to rewrite her work. Her professor won't accept this! She is contemplating how to redo her work in a short period when someone knocks on the door again.

Fuming, she dashes to the door. She rips it open, and she sees Vince holding up his fist for a knock.

"Hey…" Whatever he was supposed to say next got stuck on his throat when he saw Leanne scowling at him. What did he do? "Sweetheart?"

"Don't sweetheart me right now, Vince," he flinches at how mad she is. She even called him by his name. "I'm so close to killing you right now."

"What did I do?" he asks, frustratedly.

Instead of answering him, she turns her back to him and left him at her front door. Okay? Vince racks up his brain if he did anything that could piss her off. When he can't remember any, he decided to follow her to her room with the plastic bag that he is carrying.

After making sure that her door is locked, he follows her, stomping towards her room. When he reaches her room, he heard her mumbling.

"Stupid piece of a doorbell. The landlady said that she was going to have it fixed last week. Do I really have to repeat this? Maybe I can just edit this?"

Vince leans at her door, watching her shuffle some papers on her floor with a frown. He smiles at her scowling face and decides to make himself known.

"Mind telling me why you were mad at me a while ago?" he says, crossing sitting in front of her on the floor.

She held up a piece of paper with random chemical characters and a visible line in the middle of the paper. "See this?" She points to the line in the middle of the paper. "This happened."

"And where do I come in?" he asks, confused while staring at the paper.

"I was doing this when you suddenly knock. Since you didn't tell me that you are visiting, I wasn't prepared. This happened because I was surprised by your knock."

"I was supposed to surprise you," he defends himself.

"I was surprised, alright," she scoffs. Pulling out a clean sheet of paper and start rewriting her work. "What are you doing here, by the way?"

He grabs the paper nearest to him and sees that it a step-by-step process on how beers are manufactured. "Didn't know that you are still a student?"

"Now you know," she murmurs not looking up at him.

"What year are you in?"

"Year?" She pauses and looks up at him, confused. "I only took a one-year program for my masters."

His eyebrow rose at her. "Wow. My sweetheart is both beauty and brains."

She scoffs at his statement but smiles at how corny it is. "I doubt about the beauty and brain part. Maybe, I'll agree about you being a nerd."

He gasps mockingly, and with a high-pitched voice, he says, "Oh my. How did you know?"

She tilts her at him, annoyed. "Seriously?"

"What?" He huffs. "I was a nerd back when I was a student."

She blinks at him. "I was just joking about the nerd part a while ago. Didn't know it was true."

He grunts and lays down on the floor beside her. "I used to have braces when I was in high school. You know, the typical nerd. Books, glasses, and braces."

"So, you were always bullied?" Her assignments are forgotten as she runs her fingers through his smooth hair.

He sighs in content when she lightly scratches his scalp. "Almost, I guess. They are afraid of Deo and my father to do anything."

"Your father?"

He hums, dragging himself closer to her. "Yeah. My dad is kind of influential that no one wants to go against him. And, maybe, that's why I don't get bullied at school."

She smiles at his sleepy figure beside her. She can't help but lean in and press a kiss on his forehead. "Tell me something about your family?"

He opens his eyes and sends her a lazy smile. "Mm… I used to have a dog named Gege. But we only had for a week before we have to bring him back to the shelter."

"Why?"

"Mike, my brother, was allergic to dogs. It was so severe that he was rushed to the hospital, and Mom had to call house cleaners to clean the house spotless," He sighed at the memory. "I remember throwing a tantrum as to why Gege had to be brought back. I think I got grounded for saying the word *Fuck* for the first time that day."

She chuckles. "Bad…"

He shrugs. "I was a kid back then, and I didn't know the reason why he has to be brought back."

"When did you find out the reason why Gege was sent back?"

"The day Mike was discharged from the hospital." He looks at her. "Any fond childhood memory?"

He observes how the calm smile that was on her face slipped and change into a fake one. The warm eyes that bore into his moments ago were replaced by a faraway look as she tries to recall her childhood.

"Mm… Not sure," she answers after some time. "I don't really remember much."

She's lying. He wants to point it out, but he keeps his mouth shut as she keeps on talking. "All I know was that when I was a kid, the hospital became my second home. My health was back then-ailing to the point that I have to stay in the hospital for months on end,

"I don't really get to play much as a kid because of my health," She frowns. "But I do remember playing house with the neighbor's kids."

He abruptly sat up. "Is that kid a guy?"

She rolls her eyes at his question. "Yes, he's a guy, and I haven't seen him since forever."

"But what if you met him again…?"

She smiles at him before turning her attention back to her pending papers. "Why should I? I have my babe. It's more than enough."

Whatever jealousy Vince was feeling vanished at her admonition. A wide smile appears on his face, and as girly as it sounds, he feels giddy. He feels his face flame up in bashfulness.

My babe.

Leanne knew that Vince was blushing, and it is cute seeing him avoid eye contact with her. He clears his throat and stands up.

"I… umm… I should make us something to eat." He moves to leave her room, grabbing the plastic bag along the way.

She giggles at the way he was acting. It's good to see him fidgeting when she teases him. Her thoughts are interrupted by her phone ringing.

She frowns when she sees her brother calling her. She can't help but worry as to why he is calling. Her brother never calls her unless it was necessary, and by necessary, she meant the call he gave her four months ago to tell her that their grandmother was rushed to the hospital. And with that impression, she's hesitant in answering his call.

"Christian?"

"Annie." Her back stiffens at her brother's tone. He didn't call to ask how she is.

She made sure that she keeps her tone even. She doesn't want her brother to know that she's already on edge. "What's up?"

"Grandma's gone."

Leanne didn't understand what her brother said next with how loud the buzzing in her ear is. Her breathing became erratic, and her body became numb with the news.

It wasn't the thought of her dead grandmother that made her antsy, but what happens when someone dies. The closest thing their family ever had to a reunion.

A funeral.

It was the day of her grandfather's funeral, and there was a loud commotion outside of the funeral home her grandfather is laying rest. Leanne looked up from the sofa that she was sitting on. She was waiting for the rest of the family to finish getting ready to drive her grandfather to his final resting place when the argument outside started.

It was supposed to be a solemn day for her family, but the alarums and excursions outside filled the quiet funeral house. She tried to ignore the arguing of the elders by dragging her attention back to her book. But their voices were so loud even the guest are starting to wonder what was going on.

"You are going to stand beside the priest wearing that!" She heard her aunt yell. "You should cover yourself up, Pauline!"

"My daughter is going to wear whatever she wants!" Her uncle yelled back to his sister-in-law. "Don't tell her what to do!"

"Rome," she heard her mother speak calmly. "What Emelia means is that she's going inside a church, the House of God, we just want her to dress properly and respectfully."

However, her cousin that day decided to arrive at the funeral house wearing a white sleeveless romper short, giving her mom and aunt a heart attack. She looks like she's going to a beach party and not to deliver the homily during their grandfather's final mass.

"Pauline, you are going to a mass, not a party!" Her aunt's hands move around in agitation. "At least have some respect for your grandfather!"

At the age of sixteen, Leanne understood what her aunt was trying to say. It was the last day they get to see their grandfather before he would be buried, and the least her cousin could do is follow her aunt's request.

And what was worst, her older cousin didn't even bother to look sorry.

Fishes Swims Away and Nemo Can't be Found

She exactly has three days to prepare herself for the funeral and forty-five minutes to prepare herself for her first date.

Yes. She and Vince are going out on a date.

A lot of things had happened between the two of them, and they haven't had a proper date. She doesn't think a sleepover counts as a date.

She sighs as she glances at her monotonous wardrobe. She only has her work clothes and nothing else. She never saw the need to buy dresses or skirts, and now she's regretting her decision not to invest in one.

She grabs her phone to ask for help but then realizes that her friends are still at work, and they can't hold their phones.

As if sensing her dilemma, her phone chimes.

Vince: wear something comfortable.

She rolls her eyes at his broad statement.

She let out a low laugh upon reading his message. A day after she received the call from her brother, Vince randomly asked her out. She momentarily paused in shock, making her co-workers wonder why she suddenly paused in the hallway.

So, this is what it feels like when someone asked you out, she thought. She almost let go of her phone when he asked. She can't explain the sudden rush of excitement that course through her. The sudden onslaught of emotions in her belly was too much that she felt queasy.

Before she drops her phone on her bed, it chimes again. Thinking that it was Vince, she quickly grabs it only to find that it was her boss, approving her leave of absence.

She doesn't want to ruin her day by thinking about it, but the notification on her phone is taunting her. Should she ask Vince to accompany her?

No.

She needs to face them on her own. She's no longer that scared sixteen years old. Dr. Lynn should know about this. She made a mental note to tell her doctor tomorrow.

"Shit," she curses when she sees that she only has twenty minutes left to get ready. This is what she gets when her thoughts are scattered all over the place.

She decided to wear the first thing that she can grab on and wince when she sees how disoriented her attire is. She sighs and attempts to fix herself. She tucks her oversized shirt into her denim shorts and adds a belt for an accessory. She is transferring her belongings when her phone rings.

Just when she finally cleared her head, someone has to remind her that the happiness she was feeling was something that she just borrowed for some time. An emotion that was lent to her to cherish and cultivate, and now, it is being taken away from her.

Her thumb hovers over the green button, waiting. She let out a startled shriek when she heard the knock on the door, and the voice that was whispering to her to answer the phone disappeared. She placed it on silent. This is her day.

She hurriedly opens the door and appreciates Vince's attire. He's not wearing his glasses, making her appreciate how his eyes are like a cup of warm hot chocolate on a rainy day. His hair is neatly combed, and his shirt well ironed.

She smiles when she noticed that they both look different. She reaches up and messes with his hair.

"Hey!" He leans away from her touch and fixes his hair. "What was that for?"

"I prefer your hair unkempt." She wraps her arms around his waist and looks up at him. A wide smile made its way on her face. "Hi, babe."

Vince had to briefly compose himself when he sees her smiles. He leans in to capture her smile with his for a peck. He roams his eyes before placing kisses all over her face. She let out a shriek and laugh when he kept on pecking her face with a kiss.

"Stop," she giggles, slightly creating a distance between them without removing her arms around him.

Vince reciprocates her smile. "Hello, Sweetheart."

A warm blush rose to her face at the endearment. She clears her throat to hide the coyness that she's feeling. "So….where are we going?"

"Mm…." he says, rocking them both side to side softly. "First, we are going to have lunch because I'm starving, and then, we'll go to an aquarium to point at fishes thinking that they are all in Finding Nemo."

"Finding Nemo? Other shows have fish on them. Like Fish Hooks."

"Nah," he waves it off.

She chuckles at him. "You don't like Fish Hooks?"

"Oh! I know that show! My niece loves that show."

"Ohhh…." She wags her eyebrows at him. "Uncle Vince watches Fish Hooks."

He playfully gags at the way she's wagging her brows. "Please, don't call me that."

"And what do you prefer I call you instead?"

"Babe?" He nods, as if he was talking to somebody aside from her. "Definitely babe."

She laughs and presses a kiss on his cheeks. "Well, babe, we better get going. I can feel the anacondas in your stomach growl."

"Snakes don't growl."

She rolls her eyes at him. "They do. Occasionally."

She made sure that she had locked the door and her keys inside her bag before intertwining her fingers with Vince's.

When they reached his car, he let go of his hold on her hand to open the door for her.

"And they said chivalry is dead," she says.

"Only for you, Sweetheart," he replies before closing her door. He roundabout the car to the driver's side. "Seatbelt," he points out at which she quickly complies, but before he starts the car, he reaches for something at the passenger seat. "For you."

Leanne let out a surprised gasp when Vince hands her a bouquet of heather and lilies. "It's so beautiful. Thank you."

"Well...." He scratches his nape. "I was supposed to buy the bouquet of red roses, but you don't seem like the type to like roses—"

"I don't."

"So.... I asked the lady for a recommendation. She told me that heathers mean good luck and protection, and lilies are for purity and rebirth."

She pauses and gawks at him. He continues. "And it fits you."

Something deep inside of her awakens while he explains what the flowers mean. A deep and unknown feeling that she never knew existed. She never knew that this was what she needed. She carefully places the bouquet on her lap before turning to him.

"Thank you," she says softly. "I....well... it's my first time receiving a flower."

"And it won't be the last," he says before starting the car and silently making a mental note about bringing her flowers more often.

"Don't give me flowers every day," she gives him an annoyed look as if reading his mind. "Only during special occasions."

"But every day with you is a special occasion."

"You know what I mean."

He sighs, defeated. "Fine."

They quietly drive towards their destination. Despite the comfortable atmosphere that they have, Leanne breaks it when she keeps on feeling bothered. "Babe?"

He hums in acknowledgment. "I'll be going home."

He turns to her when they stopped by a red light. "That's good then."

She turns her head to look outside the window to hide her displeasure. "It's not."

Before he can answer her, the light turns green. He sees the restaurant that he placed a reservation in. He parks the car but doesn't cut off the engine. "What do you mean?"

She sighs and removes her seatbelt. "My brother called me yesterday telling me that our grandmother died. So, I have to go home to pay my respects."

"As you should."

He watches her shoulders drop like something heavy was placed on them. "I don't want to go."

"Why?"

"My family," she clears her throat to the clog on her throat. "My family ... they ... umm ...."

"They are the reason."

Leanne turns to look at him and see that he is staring at something far ahead. She tries to continue what she was supposed to say, but the words are stuck deep into her throat, and they refuse to get out.

Her family must have done something horrible to her, Vince thought as he cut the engine off. It must be something bad to make her scared about going home. He sighs, and before she mistakes his silence about something else, he says," Can I accompany you?"

"What?" she says, surprised at his question. She didn't expect him to speak up and volunteer himself to tag along with her.

He shrugs and glances at her. "I mean, I can ask for a week off from work to accompany you. To be your emotional support in case you needed one. What if you suddenly have an attack and I'm not there to calm you down. Wait. Does your family know about your GAD?"

She smiles and shakes her head no. "Well, that sucks," he sighs. "I can still book a ticket."

"Babe."

"Wait, let me call my substitute. See if –"

"Babe!"

"What? What?" He looks at her with wide eyes holding his phone.

She carefully places the flowers at the passenger seat before grabbing his free hand. "I'll be fine."

"Are you sure? Because I'll really company you."

She nods. "I am. I need to do this."

He sighs, defeated. "I hate it, but if you think this is what you need to do, then I'll step back. But" he held up a finger before she can say thank you. "You'll have to answer every time I'll call."

"Babe, I'm not sixteen."

"I know, but for the sake of my peace of mind," he pouts that made her giggle. "Please, sweetheart. So that I'll know that you are okay."

She rolls her eyes at his theatrics. "Fine."

"Well, then," he opens his side of the door. "Shall we continue our date? We still have to see Nemo."

Leanne: Monday 9:00 AM don't be late

Vince frowns when he sees her message to him. It was sent five minutes ago. What's on Monday? Instead of replying, he decided to wait before calling her.

She's currently on the plane to her hometown. He dropped her off at the airport that day. It's not even been thirty minutes, and he's already worried for her. He still has to wait for thirty more minutes until he can call her.

He misses her already.

He sighs. He knows that she needed this. She needed to face her demons, but he can't help but worry for her. He knows how hard it is for those who have mental issues to face their torments. He read those in books and saw them with his two eyes. That's why he wanted to accompany her. He respects her decision on going alone and that is why he's pacing back and forth in his room.

Maybe he should clean his room or do his lesson plan for class to kill the time. He glances around his room and starts picking up scattered papers. He should use his time wisely while waiting.

To not make it obvious that he was waiting, he waited for five minutes more before calling her.

One ring.

Two rings.

"Babe?"

He sighs when she answers. "You've arrived already?"

"The plane just touched down. I'm waiting for the aisle to clear up before grabbing my things."

He nods, even though she can't see him. "That's good. How are you feeling so far?"

"Mm.... Don't know. So far so good."

"You'll let me know if you start feeling anxious, okay? I don't care if it's midnight or I'm in class, just, call me."

"I will."

"See you soon?"

"Yeah. See you."

"Sweetheart?"

"Yeah?"

"I miss you."

There was a pause on the other line. "I miss you, too."

"Take care over there, okay?"

"Mmm…. Babe?"

"Yeah?"

"I… " There was an uncomfortable stillness from the other line.   "Never mind."

Before he could pry her, she had already dropped the call. Leanne's grip on her phone tightens when she realizes that she almost said the L word to him.

It wasn't the right time. She has to come out of her nightmare alive before she can utter the word to him. It's only a week. She only has to stay for a week for her grandmother's funeral.

She misses him.

She let out a deep sigh and follow the throng of people out of the plane. She sends a weak smile to the flight attendant and heads towards the arrival area. She pauses in front of the large tarpaulin with the name of her hometown.

This is it.

"You can do this," she says while patting her chest to calm down. She needs to calm herself before she left the airport. Otherwise, she's going to break down in the middle of the travel to her parent's house. "You can do this."

Your family deserved this.

She can hear him again. She's walking at a snail's pace to give her time to relax. It's been five years since she left, and she wondered how much of her hometown has changed.

"Annie!"

She glances around to find the source of the voice. Only her family calls her that. She sees her family waving at her while holding a placard with her name.

She heads towards their direction and was immediately engulfed in a hug. She let out a sigh of contentment when she smells the family scent of her mother.

"My baby girl," her mother says, cupping her face. "You're home."

She nods. Her voice refuses to work. She wants to be happy and excited that she's finally home, but she can't remove the lingering feeling of anxiousness creeping somewhere in the back of her mind.

Six days. Six more days.

For Vince.

For herself.

She can do this.

Monday couldn't have had arrived sooner, Vince thought as he stands in front of a door with a sign that says 'The Doctor is IN.'

It's been two days since Leanne left, and he will constantly call her, just to make sure that she's okay. He asked her one time what her cryptic message mean, and she just told him to go. That all of his questions will be answered when he goes to the location that she gave to him.

Imagine his shock when he sees Dr. Lynn's name on the bulletin board that was placed inside the elevator. Leanne sent him to her psychiatrist.

With a lot of questions in his mind, he knocks on the door and enters. He sees the psychiatrist sitting behind a desk, writing on a paper. She looks up when she heard the door open.

"Dr. Elepaño," she gestures to the seat in front of her. "Please make yourself comfortable."

"It's been a while since someone addressed me that," he sits on the chair in front of her table. "I kind of let them drop the honorific when I started teaching."

"Well, we are both professionals of the same field. It seems reasonable that I call you that, and I believe you are here for a reason?"

He nods. "Leanne told me to meet you today. Don't know why, though."

The doctor shook her head, stunned at what her patient did. "I always meet Lee once a month. It used to be every other week, but when I noticed some improvements, I decided to meet her once a month to check on her. I believe I'm supposed to meet her today."

"But she sent me instead," Vince felt pique at the realization.

Dr. Lynn chortles. "Now I know why she told me she'll send someone instead. How is she by the way?"

"She is hanging on. Why do you ask?"

She places both of her hands on top of her table and looks at him with acquisitive eyes. "What do you know about Leanne, Dr. Elepaño?"

He remains quiet at her question. He doesn't know anything about Leanne. Aside from the usual things he noticed about her, she hasn't opened up anything to him. About her family, her friends, or even her past.

He wants to slap himself for not knowing anything, but then he realized that all this time, he was waiting for Leanne to open up to him, to let him in, to earn her trust about the knowledge of her past. But she didn't. It made him think that she doesn't trust him at all.

"And judging from your silence, she hasn't told you anything."

He sighs and rubs his forehead when she hit the spot. "Why am I here?"

"I have the same question as you, Dr. Elepaño." Dr. Lynn leans down to grab something from her drawers. "Leanne has been my patient for two years. I was recommended to her by her company doctor."

Vince watches as she places ten notebooks in front of him. One of them was the green Starbuck planner that he was familiar with. He smiles as he remembers how he and Leanne met. It was all because of the planner that she left in

Starbucks. Who would have thought that it was almost half a year since he met Leanne, and it was one hell of a roller coaster ride?

"This planner," he chuckles under his breath as he reaches for the said planner, "started everything. Because of this planner, I met Leanne.   And because of this planner, I get to meet the person who means the world to me."

"Did you read anything from the notebook?"

Vince looks up at her and carefully places the notebook back in its place. He rubs his neck, something he would always do when he's in an uncomfortable situation and looks away guiltily. "I accidentally read a page."

"Have you told Leanne?" The doctor smirks at him.

"Oh, gods. No," He quickly sits up straighter. "Please don't tell her. I'll tell her. Oh my. She's going to bury me alive."

"Pray that she's in a great mood when you tell her."

He waves a hand at the notebooks. "Why are you asking me about that?"

"You see," Dr. Lynn smiles at him. "We both know that a person with GAD tends to keep their thoughts to themselves. I know you know that Leanne often overthinks unhealthily. There are a lot of things in her mind, from unnecessary scenarios to what she's going to eat for dinner, so, to clear her mind, I asked her to write them down.

"These notebooks are her thoughts," she hands them to him. "I believe this is the reason why she sent you here."

He tentatively held the notebook like it is fragile. It is. The notebooks are the answers to all his unanswered questions. Why now? Why did Leanne finally decide to let him in?

As he paces in his house, he keeps on asking himself if he is worth it enough to read her thoughts. He glances at the notebooks that are neatly stacked in front of him. His fingers are twitching to grab one and start reading. He sighs in defeat and grabs his phone to call Leanne.

"Hello?"

"Why?"

Leanne is taken aback by Vince's question. She excuses herself from the table and heads out to her mother's garden before answering him. "What do you mean?"

"Why, Sweetheart?"

Confused with his question, she starts to play around her mother's rose bushes, and then it struck her. It's Monday.

"Oh, shit," she murmurs. She suddenly wants to become one of her mother's flowers when she remembers the reason why she wanted him to see Dr. Lynn. "Umm… So, what did Dr. Lynn say?"

"I don't have to read these if it makes you uncomfortable, Sweetheart."

This is why she fell for Vince. He always prioritizes her. Her thoughts. Her feelings. He makes her feel like she's someone important.

She's used to be the one who's always invisible, the one who always hides in the corner. She always prefers that, to have the spotlight away from her. She never knew what it felt like to have someone see her when she's wallpaper, and to have someone actually see her in the corner is flattering and heartwarming.

"No," she says with a lot of conviction in her tone. "I know you have a lot of questions, and those answers are in those notebooks. This is the only way I can think of for you to know me. The real me. And I will definitely chicken out if I do this face to face."

Vince stops his pacing and lets out a relieved sigh. He doesn't know why he was so worked up while talking to Leanne.

"I just hope that the moment you finish reading the notebooks, whatever feelings you have of me won't change. That I'll still be your sweetheart."

He smiles when he hears the fuss in her tone. "I miss you already."

Leanne smiles. "I miss you, too."

"So, how's the family reunion?"

She rolls her eyes at his question before dropping herself beside the bushes. "My grandma's burial is tomorrow. The rest of our relatives will arrive today."

"How are you feeling so far?"

"Nothing yet." She shrugs. "Nothing to be worried about. Yet."

"Sweetheart…"

She sighs. She hates it when he uses that tone on her. He knows when she's bullshitting him. She can't lie to him. "I had a mini-breakdown when I arrived here yesterday."

Vince sighed in frustration. Why does she have to be so far away from him? He hates this feeling of loneliness and irritation at their distance. He aches to have her beside him. His arms twitch as he held the urge to reach through the phone to hug her. He wants to be where she is right now to comfort her.

"But I'm fine now," she quickly cut off his thoughts. She doesn't want him to worry about her wellbeing. "Talking to you actually helps."

"Glad to be of service."

She giggles before glancing back when she heard the door of the garden open and see both of her brothers' heads peak out of it. Christian opens the door wider, and the two of them made themselves comfortable beside her.

"Sweetheart?"

She sees her brothers tilt their heads when they heard Vince's endearment for her. They are going to interrogate her the moment she ends the call.

"Yeah?"

"I miss you."

She ignores her brothers and smiles at no one. It was the second time he told her that. And she's not against it. "Me too, Babe."

"Talk to you later?"

"Yeah. Take care."

"I love you."

Vince pauses when he realizes what he just said. He told Leanne that he loves her, and the way he said those words are so smooth and familiar, like those words were meant to be uttered by him and to be heard by Leanne.

He glances at his phone and feels crestfallen when he didn't receive a message from Leanne about his words. He sighs and drops himself on the floor. Kutch takes that opportunity to rub himself on his leg.

"Do you think I scared her?" he asks the cat, who looks at him blankly. "Did I say it too soon?"

He groans. He's asking a cat for guidance. He's so fucked. He opted to start reading the notebooks again before he loses his mind about what happened.

Meanwhile, Leanne was dumbstruck by what Vince said before he drops the call. He loves her.

I love you.

And when he utters the words, they feel familiar. It was so sophisticated, and she likes the way those words made her feel. She feels a big heavy burden was lifted from her when he said those words. She thought that it would be one-sided love, but Vince proved her wrong. Like he always does.

She presses her phone to her lips to stop herself from squealing, but the happiness that she is feeling is too overwhelming that the smile that she was trying to hide broke free. The smile turns into a giggle, and the giggle turns into laughter until she is burying her face at her palms to hide her red face.

She is so happy that Vince loves her. She is so happy that she even hugs her brothers. She is so happy that she has to calm herself down as her heartbeat became erratic. It is pounding so loud that she can hear it in her ears.

When she finally calms herself down, she let out a sigh and lay on the grass. She knows her brothers wanted to ask her questions, and she's in a really good mood. So, she enlightens them.

"Go on," she turns her head to look at them. "I know you are dying to know."

"Wait," Michael holds up a hand in front of her. "You are dating someone?"

She nods, smiling. "Woah," he is blown away with that new information. "Who is he? What's his work? How did you two meet?"

"And you let him call you sweetheart?" Christian asks, still trying to wrap his mind about his sister dating someone.

Leanne just smiles at their question and closes her eyes to let the warmth of the midmorning sun embrace her. The ray of the sun stings her skin a bit, but she ignores it as she was heady with unexplainable happiness.

"Shit."

She stiffens at her brother's tone. She slowly opens her eyes hoping that those few seconds will give her the courage that she needs.

"Are they here?" she whispers to her brother with her eyes wide open while staring at the blue skies.

"Just Rome and Ernie," Michael says, pulling himself up. "I should head in and make sure that Ma doesn't interact with them alone. Let alone with my wife."

She frowns when she recalls that certain event. From then on, she and her brothers made sure that if their uncles are around, their mother shouldn't be alone.

Seeing her mother cry more than once because of their uncles is enough for them to draw the line. It really amazes her how her mother's older brothers have the guts to face them after what they did to her family.

"I'll stay here for a little while," she says, closing her eyes again. Delaying the inevitable.

"You'll be fine here alone?" Michael asks her following Christian's actions. He is slightly worried at his sister's pale complexion.

She nods, pushing down the anxiety that's climbing her throat. She can feel her chest starting to burn due to nausea and her stomach urging her to vomit her breakfast.

"I thought they'll be here by noon?" She hears Michael ask Christian as they head back inside her parents' house.

She thought the same thing. She takes a deep breath and inhales the fresh scent of the flowers that are surrounding her. She suddenly remembers the flowers that Vince gave to her. Lilies and Heather.

Death and Protection.

Purity and Admiration.

Fresh life and Good Luck.

She doesn't know what Vince was trying to convey to her then, but she doesn't really care. She has to face her past first before seeing the future with Vince.

With that thought in mind, Leanne pulls herself up from where she's hiding and stretches her muscles before following her brothers. It was after, all the time to face the music that she's been avoiding.

Leanne doesn't know that she's been staring at the open door until her cousin calls her out.

"You okay there?" her maternal cousin, Marie, asks her with her daughter holding her hand. "You've been staring."

She clears her throat to push down the embarrassment that she feels for being caught. "Yeah, I'm just trying to get a bit of strength before facing them."

Her cousin frowns when she realizes what she meant. "It's a war zone. They didn't wait for the kids to leave before sputtering bullshit. I have to ask Michael to bring the kids to our room to be away from this. We've been traumatized enough for this. I don't want the kids to experience it too."

"Mama said a bad word," Marie's daughter says, quietly.

Her cousin pats her daughter's head. "I'm sorry, baby. Don't repeat what Mama said."

"Okay," she agreed right away and continue to hide behind her mother's legs.

Leanne wants to chuckle at the mother-daughter interaction but can feel her anxiety growing, and she's trying to push it aside. She subtly wipes her sweating hands on her jeans. She glances at her cousin's youngest and sees that she's hiding behind her mother. "Mom's garden is quiet. It's also far away from them."

"Thank you," Marie smiles at her cousin. She calls her attention before leaving her at the door. "Annie?"

"Yeah?"

"Don't let them get to you."

She stiffens at her cousin's words before she leaves her alone by the door. She let out a sigh and shut the door. Her hands are twitching to call Vince and ask for help, but a part of her is reprimanding her for depending on Vince. This is something that she has to do alone. Dragging Vince into this won't do her any good. It might even worsen her condition.

"You can do this," she murmurs as he slowly walks towards the living room where her relatives are. "You can do this."

As she makes her way towards the kitchen, she can hear their loud voices. The moment she heard their voices, she pauses at the archway that separates the living room from the dining room. Their voices remind her of the reason why she left in the first place. As she why she chose the cowards way out.

"I know our mother left us something." She heard her uncle says. "Don't be selfish and share it! It was for the five of us."

Money can make a person greedy. That's what happened to her three uncles, who are currently bullying her mother. She remembered her late grandma saying that money is the root of all evil, and she's right. Her grandmother saw how money changed her three sons. She saw what money can do to her family. It controls and destroys everything you cherished.

Her uncles let money control their life, making them greedy and assholes. They bullied her family because of money when all her family did was lend them a hand. Instead of being grateful to her mother, they turn their backs to her and stab her repeatedly until she's battered and broken.

Her mother, the subject of their wretched attitude, had shed so many tears because of them, and her family has been brittle since then. They were forced to move from one place to another until she was able to graduate and leave.

She helped build the home where her parents are currently staying. She wants them to be far away from them as much as possible. But her mother refused to say that she grew up in that place and she'll die in that place, whereas Leanne wanted nothing to do with her hometown. It brought too much pain and trauma for her.

Leanne shrugs the thoughts away and takes a deep breath before heading towards the living room. She moves quietly so that they wouldn't notice her, but to her dismay, her uncle Ernie noticed her.

"Why don't you ask your daughter?" He turns the spotlight to her. "She's wealthy enough for this family. We just want our share of the inheritance."

"Leave my daughter out of this, Ernie!" Her mother yells while Leanne cowers away from their sight. "She worked hard for her wealth, and never once did we lend her anything."

Leanne wants to speak up for herself, but the loud ringing in her ears made her step back. The anxiety she was trying to calm slowly starts to creep up her chest, making it burn and harder to breathe. She places a shaky hand on her chest and taps it softly.

Calm down.

Calm down.

Calm down.

She tries to upright herself making it seem like there is nothing wrong with her but her sweaty and shaky hands say a different thing. Her anxiety is slowly crawling at her throat. She silently reprimands herself to calm down. Otherwise, she's going to hurl her breakfast at her mother's newly washed carpet.

"Why can't I ask for my share?" Rome asks in a loud tone. "Just admit it that you want to have all the inheritance to yourself!"

"What inheritance are you talking about, Rome?" Her aunt Emelia ask Rome. "There is no inheritance."

"What the fuck are you talking about?" Ronald, the second eldest, asked. "There is!"

Just like her three uncles, Leanne was stunned by the news her aunt dropped. Along with the sudden news, her anxiety dissipates for a while, making her consciousness clear.

"Mother sold the house, Ron," her mother explains. "Along with the lands that Father left to her. She needed the money for her hospitalization. Our savings weren't enough to cover her medical and hospital bills."

"Why the fuck did you sell the lands?" Ernie bellows, closing the distance between him and her mother, ignoring her mother's explanation. "It's our land! Father left it to us! No one has the right to sell it but us!"

Everything that happened next was in slow motion and a reenactment of the memory that she kept hidden from everyone. She watches Ernie raise his hand towards her mother, making a move to hit her and she remains rooted on her spot near the wall. However, instead of seeing her mother, she sees a sixteen-year-old Michael on the ground in front of her uncle, weeping from the punch that he received from the latter.

Just like what happened then, Leanne just stood there like a statue. She wanted to walk towards her brother, to protect him, but she was so scared at what her uncle did to her brother that her body froze. She was so scared to even cry as she watched her brother whimper, holding his stomach. She didn't know how long she had been standing there waiting for this to be over. A few minutes later, when she slowly had her bearing, she tentatively approached her brother, who fainted from the pain.

She let out the cry that refused to show moments ago. "I'm sorry," she chanted all over again and again as she cradled her brother's body to hers.

She's the eldest among them. It was her job to protect her younger brothers, but at that time, Leanne never felt so helpless and useless for not protecting her brother. It was one of the reasons why she left. The guilt had been gnawing at her for years. Eating her consciousness slowly day by day. Michael might have forgiven her, but she can never forgive herself for letting that happen to him.

"THAT'S ENOUGH!"

A loud voice bellows, and Leanne realizes that it came from her. She looks up and sees everyone staring at her. She doesn't know where she got the strength and the courage to yell. She can feel her insides churning at the attention that she's receiving, but she schools her expression and made sure that they don't sense her fear.

She's no longer seeing her brother on the floor but her mother, who is about to be hit by her uncle. She sees her father pull her mother away from her uncle as their attention were occupied with her.

"Don't you think it's time to forgive yourself?" She can hear Dr. Lynn's questions during their session.

"I don't think I can," she looked down at her lap, ashamed of her admittance. "I can still see him hitting my brother, and at night where it is the most silent, I can hear my brother's pained whimpering. I was supposed to protect him, but I didn't because I was scared. If you were in my shoes then, what will you do?"

Instead of answering her, Dr. Lynn asked her a question. "Have you told your parents about this incident?"

"Why should I?" she said, repulsed at the thought of her parents knowing. They already had enough on their plate, and she and her brother agreed to not let their family know.

"Lee, it's okay to be scared sometimes and—"

"You don't get it!" she burst. "I'm the eldest! It's my job to protect my brother, my family, but what did I do? I just stood there and did nothing. I can't even protect him then. What made you think that I can protect him now?"

"I think the reason why you can't forgive yourself is that you refused to, or you want to protect something dear to you to suffice the guilt that's eating you. But one way or the other, you have to let go of your guilt. You can't protect everyone, Lee."

What Dr. Lynn said to her then slowly made sense as her mother is a few safe spaces away from her uncle. She can feel the guilt that she's carrying for years, slowly loosening their hold on her. To be able to stop her uncle from hitting her mother was what she needed. It was something that she wasn't able to do then, but now she's a different person, and she refuses to let anyone dear to her get hurt again.

"How dare you raise your voice at me?!" Ernie yells at her. "Did your parents teach you to respect your elders?"

She raises her chin and hides her shaking hands in her pockets to hide them from him. "Respect should be earned, not forced. I learned that much from them."

"You little—" Rome moves towards her.

"I suggest you don't raise your hand at me," she glares at them. "I have a sister-in-law who works with the law, and she won't hesitate to throw you in jail for hitting me, or my Mama."

"How dare you talk back to your elders." Her uncle Ronald says, his face beet red from anger.

"How dare I?" She scoffs. "How dare you try to hit my mama in her home. You have the guts to demand and bully her in her own home. You are just visitors here. If you can't respect my mama in her own home, at least respect grandma."

"Ungrateful little bitch!" She can see Ernie move to hit her but Christian block him from approaching her.

"I suggest you think twice about what you are about to do," he seethes before tilting his head to the side to where the rest of their relatives are. "Your grandchildren are watching."

Her uncle forcefully removes his hand from her brother and leaves the room with his wife and kids in tow, but before he can leave the door, her sister-in-law calls him.

"I'm filing a restraining order against the three of you and the rest of your families for threatening and harassment," she says, cuddling her newborn child closer to her chest. "Expect a call anytime soon."

Embarrassed at how the events have turned, the rest of her uncles left, with Ernie leaving her, her family, and her mother's older brother's family in the living room. When they heard the last car leave, only then did they let out a deep sigh of relief while Leanne drops on the floor. She finally did it. She's finally able to protect her family.

Vince takes his time in reading Leanne's notebooks. Scared to lost one of them. He only read them when he's at home. So far, he had finished reading two of her notebooks, and he can't explain what he was supposed to feel as he flip from one page to another.

"Professor Elepaño."

He turns his attention to his student who is raising her hand. "Yes?"

"Are you single?"

He laughs alongside the rest of the class at her question. He leans his body on the table as if he was thinking about how to answer her question. "In terms of my documents, I'm single."

He hears a series of squeals, mostly from his female students. "However, I'm no longer on the market. My sweetheart would be jealous."

The reactions were a mixture of 'awws' and 'damn'. He calls out the kid at the far back who was raising his hand.

"How long have you been in a relationship with your sweetheart?"

"It hasn't been a year since I've known her," he shrugs. "And only a month or less since we made it official. I think?"

"So, we actually have a chance?"

He glances at the student who said the question. "I worked hard to earn her trust and to get to know the real her. I don't think what I feel for her would be that shallow or something that can easily be destroyed. And I hope that you will be able to meet someone like how I met my sweetheart."

After answering a few more questions that aren't related to his class, he dismissed them early. He is fixing his table when he sees that Leanne is calling him.

"Hello, Sweetheart."

"I love you."

Vince pauses at what he hears. Did she say the word? His elation is replaced with worry at how breathless she sounded.

"Sweetheart?" He ignores his table and move to close the door for privacy. "Are you okay?"

"I love you, Vince. So much."

She ignores his question. Vince let out a chuckle at what she said and rub his neck when he feels his face redden at the elated emotion that he is suppressing. It made him miss her more.

"Well, damn," he grunts. "I wish you were here."

"Two more days, Babe. Two more days."

He leans on his table, with the widest smile on his face. "Want me to fetch you from the airport?"

Leanne murmurs her agreement. "I miss you."

"Me too, Sweetheart."

"I did it, Babe."

"Of what?" he asks, confuse at what she's referring.

"I beat my demons."

Vince pats his chest when he feels it beating harden with happiness and excitement for her. "I know you can do it. Want to tell me how it happened?"

He kept quiet as Leanne narrate everything that happened in her parent's house. He knew much about her family based on her notebooks, but to hear her recount everything without breaking down, Vince feels like a proud parent.

She's finally free of her demons. She can finally spread her wings.

And he's so in love with her.

He didn't know how long they'd been talking until the door opens and a student peeps his head inside, signaling him that it was time for his next class.

"Sweetheart, it's time for my next class," he reluctantly says.

"Oh," he can hear the disappointment in her tone. "Talk to you later?"

"Will do."

"Vince?"

"Yeah?"

"I love you."

Vince doesn't bother in hiding the big smile that appears on his face which made his student tease him. "I love you too. Take care, okay?"

She laughs at the teasing Vince is experiencing from his students. "I will."

Vince waits for her to end the call and turn to his class. "Anyone ready for the quiz?"

"Thank you for boarding with us. Hope you had enjoyed your travel with us. Have a safe day."

Leanne impatiently waits as the crowd slowly disperse before she stands up and grabs her bag. She may have recovered a part of her but being in a crowd still makes her uncomfortable.

Remembering that Vince is supposed to fetch her, she hastens her steps towards the exit. A week without him was intolerable. She got used to his touch and smell that a week without him was hell. She hopes that this will be the last time that they are going to be separated this long. She scans the crowd for his familiar build but slowly deflates that she can't see his silhouette anywhere.

She grabs her phone from her bag. Her plane was delayed for half an hour, but she made sure to relay the news to him.

Did he got stuck in traffic?

Or he forgot?

Leann frowns at the last thought before calling Vince's number. She hears it ring somewhere near her. She glances around once more, and she felt her shoulders drop in relief when she sees him a few meters away from her, holding a bouquet of lilies and heathers just like the bouquet he first gave her.

Ecstatic to see him, Leanne ignores her social anxiety and runs towards Vince's open arms, who captures her when she slams herself to him for a hug.

The scent of lemon and mint engulf her senses making everything around her disappear, and as of the moment, she doesn't care if everyone was staring at them. All that matters then was that she's finally in Vince's arms.

She's finally home.

She's finally where she should be.

"I miss you," Vince grunts, tightening his arms around her and pressing a kiss to her temple.

She buries her face deeper into his neck and inhales his addicting scent. "I miss you too."

As much as he likes their position, he has to make sure of something first. "What you said on the phone, do you mean it? Because, Sweetheart, if you are playing with those words..."

Whatever words Vince was supposed to say next disappears when Leanne reaches up and presses her lips to his to silence his babbling. She made sure to convey everything she felt for Vince in that kiss that the doubt that he was feeling a while ago dissipate.

All rational thoughts left Vince's thoughts when Leanne's soft lips press to his. He doesn't care if they are displaying too much affection. All that mattered to him was only Leanne. Like his lips knew exactly what to do, he returned the kiss in the same ferocity as Leanne's. He pulls her closer to his body like it wasn't enough. Holding her is no longer enough to suffice his love and hunger for her. Everything he does for her is not enough to tell her that he loves her. She deserves more, and he's willing to give his all in this.

When the need to breathe came, Leanne groans her frustration when Vince lets go of her lips to press a warm and sweet kiss to her forehead.

He cups her face and tilts it up to face him. With his eyes on her and with conviction, he says the words to her intimately. "I love you. So damn much."

Leanne smiles at him and hold his hands. "I love you too. So damn much."

He let out a chuckle when she repeated what he said before he can lean in to press a kiss on her lips again when a voice suddenly interrupts them.

"I'm happy to see my sister finally dating someone, but I do hope you two realize that you are eating each other's faces in public."

Leanne suddenly pushes herself away from him and turns to the owner of the voice. He frowns when she left his embrace. He turns to glare at the person when he came face to face with Leanne's family. They were all looking at them with knowing grins on their faces except for a man and a woman who is glaring at Leanne.

He can see Leanne as he keeps on staring at her family. He then stiffens when a certain weight is dropped on him when her father's attention turns to him.

"I suggest you start introducing us, Annie, before Mama and Papa kill your boyfriend."

Leanne can feel a blush is starting to form on her face at how her brother describes Vince. Is that what they are? Nobody had popped the question regarding that, but the warm feeling that engulf her at the thought of Vince being her boyfriend made her blissful.

"Babe," she holds his hand and introduces him to her family. Pointing out who is who as she goes. "This is Christian, the youngest and his fiancée. Michael, who is two years younger than me, and his wife. This is my Mama and Papa. Everyone, Vince, my boyfriend."

"Oh, we know," her brother, Michael chuckle which earned him a slap from his wife. "What?"

"Behave," she hisses at her husband.

Vince let out a silent gulp when her father walk towards him. "What is it that you do?"

"Pa!" Leanne is appalled at her father's question, but she keeps her mouth shut when he raises a hand in her direction.

"I'm talking to him, Annie," he says in the tone that scares her when she was a child. He directs the question to Vince. "What it is that you do?"

"I'm a professor, sir," Vince says. She wants to laugh at how stiff he is but keeps it all in her mind.

Her father raises an eyebrow. "Oh, a stable income?"

He nods. "I do."

"You think you can handle my daughter?"

He tightens his hold on her hand. "I do, sir."

Her dad stares at him from head to toe before turning his back to him. "Will you be joining us for lunch?"

Leanne glances at Vince smiling while he tips his head in her direction in acknowledgment. "Yes, Sir. I will be."

Her father grunts in answer while Leanne buries her face in his arm. "My Papa like you already."

"You think so?" he asks, skeptical.

"Man," her brother, Christian, says. Overhearing his question. "He invited you to lunch. That should mean something, right?"

He felt like the huge chuck of weight was removed from his chest at Christian's explanation. It means a lot to him to have the favor of Leanne's family since he doesn't plan on letting go of her.

"Vince, right?"

He turns to Leanne's mother. "Yes, Ma'am."

She smiles at him and gently pats his cheek. She turns to Leanne's brothers. "Let's get going. Boys, grab the luggage."

What was that? He turns his gaze to Leanne, who tiptoes and presses a kiss on his cheek. Secretly, laughing at his perplexed expression. "Let's go, Babe. We don't want to make my parents wait."

What...?

09/07/2019

I got promoted.

It sucks.

leave

9/11/2019

I hate my thoughts right now. I hate that I'm having suicidal thoughts. (I mostly have it when my anxiety attacks when I'm alone.) I hate it when I have sleep paralysis. Everyday. I hate it. I hate it. I hate it. Really hate it. I hate myself for being insane. I really do.

I want out.

                                        leanne

11/11/2020

if this is what ~~if~~ it feels like to be heartbroken
then I'm not in a relationship. It sucks
when someone breaks your trust over and over
again. I bet that I'm ~~struck~~ scared to face my
problems head on. I hate this attitude of
mine. I want out.

To whom this ~~little~~ note may concern,

Okay. How to start this? Right, you want to know what's in my head, right? You want to know what I'm thinking or feeling right now, right? Well to tell you I feel like shit.

They said that to ease the burden you have or rather need some one to talk to. well, that is not the case for me. In order to carry any burden, I write it down and I'll be fine the next day. And for you to be able to read this really speaks a lot for me cause I'm really uncomfortable right now and requires a lot of alcohol in order to write this) and to you because (I trust you more than my parents. You read that right)

Leanne
02/09/2020

3/14/2021

I have a fight with my parents. My parents don't even know what I'm thinking most of the time. even after I left home. My mother cried upon knowing that I have [illegible] and I have to undergo [illegible]. this is why I don't tell them anything.

pardon for my penmanship. Speaking of that my story will start at the day my grandpa died. Everything became shit when he died. I'm really hoping that I'll be okay and accept after this. this is embarrassing to read again

Leanne

1/27/2022

I saw him again and I like the warm feeling that he gave me. I like what his presence is to me. It gave me hope that I can actually survive the world. that I can do everything.

Brianna